Son of a Gun

To the despair of wealthy rancher Harry Grant, his teenage son, Hal, is hanging out with a bunch of wrong 'uns. But it's when the Percys arrive on the Big G range with a herd of longhorns that the real trouble begins.

The Percys decide to settle on Grant's land and, to aid them in fending off an eviction order, send for their cousins – the Mortimers – a clan of outlaws notorious for their cold-blooded brutality.

Hal is sucked into the vicious family feud when he meets and falls for beautiful Morgan Percy. Now he must decide where his loyalties lie and prove whether he is man enough to go up against the fearsome combination of killers and outlaws.

Son of a Gun

Elliot James

A Black Horse Western

ROBERT HALE · LONDON

ISBN-10: 0-7090-7977-X
ISBN-13: 978-0-7090-7977-4

Robert Hale Limited
Clerkenwell House
Clerkenwell Green
London EC1R 0HT

To my IT men
Mick French and Giles Richardson

Typeset by Derek Doyle & Associates, Shaw Heath.
Printed and bound in Great Britain by
Antony Rowe Limited, Wiltshire.

1

Harrison Percy rode through the dust with his eyes almost shut. He had pulled his bandanna over his mouth and nose in a vain attempt to screen out the fine dust kicked up by the spooked herd. Somewhere up ahead was his father Tom Percy, tracking the herd as were the rest of the trail hands.

There was nothing to be done now only follow behind the herd. That they would eventually run out of steam was a certainty. The crew could do no more than follow the dust and the wide swathe of trampled earth and at the end the herd would be there. Scattered they might be but the steers would tend to bunch together and run until exhausted or a natural barrier would halt them.

Once they had caught up, his boys would bring the herd together. The rampaging steers would do some damage but that was to be expected. He just hoped the herd itself would not sustain serious injury.

The migration north was born of necessity. Three dry years had devastated the grasslands of Exton County. The herds of longhorns built up over the years had dwindled drastically. His father had called him in one day.

'Son, I reckon we have to go in search of water. This land is becoming a desert. If'n we stay another season we won't have a cattle business worth a coyote's droppin's. I counted another five carcasses in the last few days.'

'I guess you're right. Sure is grievous hurtful to see them steers suffer so.' Harrison had shook his head ruefully. 'Sure will be hard to pull up stakes an' move on from here.' He had rubbed his thick, close-cropped, red beard. 'Cain't help remembering I grew up here, learnt cow punchin' from you. It's a hard thing to do but cain't see no other way.'

Sometime in the early morning the herd had spooked. No one would know exactly why. It could have been as simple as a rattler, or wolves, or some such predator. Now the trail hands could only drag along in the wake of the herd and hope they did not lose too many beasts in the mêlée.

As the dust became less dense he could see other mounted figures. He spurred toward them.

'Howdy,' he yelled out.

The riders turned towards him. They raised a hand in greeting. It was hard to tell who was who under the coating of dust. One of the riders pulled down his bandanna.

'Howdy, son. Pete reckons there's a town up ahead apiece. Just hope the herd missed it. Anyways might as well stop for a drink and a break. Sure don't do a man's throat no good suckin' dust.'

They rode into Lourdes and looked no further than the Hot Spur saloon. It was right on the main drag. Wearily they pushed up to the garishly painted building advertising beer, whiskey, women and song.

There were ten of them by now as they gathered up

stragglers from the original herders. A couple of riders were missing but until they knew any better those men were probably still trailing the herd.

'Set 'em up. Beers OK, you fellas?'

Heads nodded all around as the thirsty men bellied up to the bar.

'The herd came through here,' Tom whispered, out of the corner of his mouth.

Harrison nodded. 'I saw the smashed wagons an' hitchin' rails as well as some o' the boardwalk broken. Anyone asks, act dumb. We're just passin' through.'

Foaming beers were lined up in front of the cowboys. Glasses tipped in the air and took only seconds to empty.

'Set 'em up again,' Tom called, setting down his money. 'That didn't even wet m' tongue.'

The patrons of the big saloon were eyeing the dusty 'punchers at the bar. Harrison knew it would not take them long to put two and two together and connect them with the runaway herd. As if to confirm his thoughts the batwings burst open and several townsmen entered. At their head was a large, bowler-hatted man.

With his battered face he looked like a pugilist. Indeed Bill Gristy still travelled to the big bouts and fought for sizeable prize monies. He ran a notorious gambling den in Hide Town, so called because of the number of bare-fleshed women plying their trade in the area.

Bristling with aggression, Gristy stood straddle-legged and glared at the row of cowboys with the beer tankards.

'You the cowpokes 'long them ponies out there?'

'What's it to yuh?' Harrison said over his shoulder without turning his head. 'I don't know about you boys, but this here beer ain't yet shifted the dust on m' tonsils.'

As well as being punched out of shape, Gristy's face was a beefy red. If possible it became even more livid at this snub.

'Damn your eyes . . .' Gristy grabbed the young puncher by the shoulder and spun him round.

As he came round, Harrison smashed the tankard into Gristy's face. Broken glass and beer cascaded down the big man's front. Harrison then drove his knee up into the pugilist's groin. He followed this with a hard punch into the man's midriff. Gristy staggered back a few paces but did not go down under this attack. Harrison shook his head.

'Gawddamn tough ole bastard this.'

Gristy was bent double, holding on to his injured lower parts. A dusty boot smashed into his teeth and he was flung over on to his back and lay gasping like a landed fish. Blood seeped from his gashed face and dripped on to the sawdust of the saloon floor.

Harrison walked across to the group of men who had followed Gristy into the saloon.

'Tell your friend, when he's in a state to listen, to be a mite more polite to strangers. I've known men git killed for less'n what he did. I don't like to be mauled around. Certainly not by a big, ugly gorilla wearing store-bought clothes.'

The townsfolk shifted uneasily under the hard-eyed gaze of the bearded youngster.

Behind the cowpoke, Gristy rolled over on to his front and began the laborious process of pushing himself on to all fours. Harrison turned and viciously kicked the big man in the side of the head. Gristy tumbled on to the sawdust once more and decided to stay there.

'He'll kill you for sure,' one of the men ventured.

'That there is Bill Gristy. Sure as shootin' he'll come after you.'

'Wa-al, I ain't never heard of no Mr Bill Gristy. He's mebbe a big man in this two-bit town. If'n he wants to know who it was put him in the sawdust, the name is Harrison Percy. Tell him next time he wants to tussle with me he won't git off so lightly.' He turned to his men standing at the bar with empty beer glasses. 'You fellas ready to ride?'

'Sure boss,' came the chorus.

'Let's hit the trail then. There's a bunch of cows out there feeling kinda lonely an' neglected.' Harrison grinned at Tom Percy. 'Guess this town'll not fergit us in a hurry.'

Tom grinned back at his son, the light of pride shining in his eyes. 'Gawddamn, I sure raised you right well. You're one helluva son of a gun.'

With yells of sheer exuberance the trail hands elbowed their way past the stunned townsfolk. The saloon remained silent as the clamour of the cowpunchers faded along with the hoof beats of their ponies as the strangers exited the town.

2

The drumbeat in Hal Grant's head woke him. He groaned and rolled over, then wished he had kept still. The room seemed to be revolving. A steady vibration of snoring drew his attention.

Nearby, lying on a table was a large man. He was lying on his back and it was he who filled the air with turbulent noise as he breathed stertoriously in whiskey-fuelled slumber.

Hal shuddered and tried to sit up. It took him a few moments fighting the dizziness that threatened to overwhelm him before he was properly upright.

'Never again,' he moaned, as he sat hunched over holding his pounding head in his hands. He got to his feet and, swaying unsteadily, made his way to the window and opened the shutters. Bright sunlight burst into the room. Hal cursed and hastily shut his eyes as the brilliant sun flared into the room.

'Son of a bitch,' he groaned, and let go the shutter. It swung on rusty hinges and banged noisily against the wall. Hal turned away from the window in time to see the big man cease snoring and cautiously open one eye.

'Hal? Hal, is that you makin' that dang blasted noise?'

The youngster did not answer. The big man sat up and, like his, companion groaned and put his hands to his head.

'Call up Madam Quigley, Hal. I need a drink. Dang blasted head. Need a hair o' the dawg.'

'Call her yourself, you fat tub of lard. If'n I call out my head'll split wide open.'

The fat man groaned lustily and then belched noisily.

'Gawddamn it, Hal, you ought to be more respectful to a man of my dignity. That's the trouble with young-sters nowadays. No respect for their elders!' The fat man groaned again for effect. 'Aw, what a night! I lost count of the bottles of whiskey we downed. We had the legs of Madam Quigley run off'n her keepin' us replenished.' He stood unsteadily and waddled to the door. 'Madam Quigley, Madam Quigley,' he called banging a fist on the door. 'Oh, my achin' head!' He came and sat down again.

'Hal, when you take over the Big G, don't fergit who it was taught you to swill whiskey an' bed wenches.'

'Wa-al, I suppose if'n I had to be shown how to be a wastrel I couldn't a picked a better teacher than ole Jack Falmouth.'

'Ain't that the truth!' the big man said complacently. 'An' the mistress of the Mule's Head, Madam Quigley, keeps a most depraved house for your edification.'

'I guess a bear likes honey just as a buffalo likes grass,' the younger man interjected.

'You're in a strange mood. What the hell have I got to do with bears and buffaloes?'

'An' what the hell have I got to do with the madam of

a bawdy house, I asks you?' Hal answered.

'You used the services of the house aplenty.'

Hal looked at the fat man and frowned. 'So! I allus paid my way,' he retorted.

'I'll give you that. I never had to pay your tab. Mind you, there is the wealth of the Big G behind you,' Falmouth said, then added thoughtfully. 'By the way, Hal, when you're boss of the Big G will you hang thieves and rustlers?'

'No, but you can.' Hall grinned across at the fat man.

'Oooh, I don't rightly know as how I could put a necktie on a friend. All my acquaintances are villains.' Falmouth made a wry face and caressed his neck seemingly disturbed by the thought. 'By the way,' he continued, brightening, 'I braced the banker the other day for a loan. The miserable toad tole me he wouldn't encourage an ole reprobate like me and berated me for misleadin' the youth of the town.' Falmouth cast a sly glance at Hal. 'He seemed a mite concerned about you, Hal. Said as how he couldn't see what good it would do you hangin' round with a rake like myself.'

Hal looked speculatively at his companion.

'You did well to git to see the manager of the bank. I would have thought he wouldn't let you over the threshold.'

'I met him in the street.'

'You braced him in the street! What'd you do anyway? Invite him down to Madam Quigley for a quiet game of poker? No, I reckon not. Even you wouldn't be that dumb.'

'It's all your fault, Hal. Before I met you I was of good character. I was never a wrong 'un. Now a rancher's son has damned me.'

Hal tried to smother his amusement, but lolled back against the table and chortled aloud. Eventually he sat up and looked around confidentially before speaking. 'I know where there's a few steers wandered in a gully and missed the branding iron.' He winked broadly at his companion.

Falmouth's eyes brightened. 'You have a plan to rustle them, Hal? Count me in.'

'I see you're like a cow's tail blowing in the wind. You go quickly from remorse to rustlin'.'

'Why, Hal, I need this work. It's my line of business,' Falmouth retorted peevishly. He went to the door and banged loudly. 'Madam Quigley! Madam Quigley! Is everyone deef or dead in this house!'

Just then a tall, handsome woman entered carrying a tray. When she set the tray down there was the sound of mugs rattling together. The smell of strong coffee began to permeate the stale, smoky atmosphere of the room.

'Madam Quigley, you enter like a queen bearin' gifts to your humble subjects,' Falmouth gallantly pronounced. 'Is that coffee I smell? Coffee is for the lower classes. I on the other hand require beverage of a stronger nature. Did you not bring nectar of the gods for thirstin' gentry?'

'I might have known, Jack Falmouth, that coffee wouldn't satisfy you.' Madam Quigley produced a whiskey bottle from her skirt pocket and thumped it on to the table beside the fat man. She smiled over at the younger man. 'Hal will 'preciate a cup of coffee an' a plate of flapjacks.'

Hal grinned back at the woman. 'I could eat a boiled

calf right now but a few flapjacks will do just as well.'

Madam Quigley sat at a table and pulled out a small cigar and lit it. She sat puffing clouds of smoke, fondly watching Hal as he poured coffee and started on the flapjacks. Then she switched her attention to Falmouth who was now sitting swigging directly from the neck of the whiskey bottle. 'Are you in need of employment, Jack?'

Falmouth burped loudly. 'Pardon, ma'am, depends on what you have in mind.'

'My girls tell me a certain party starts out tomorrow for Toska with a well-filled money belt.'

Cradling the whiskey bottle in his arms, Falmouth eyed the owner of the saloon speculatively. 'That is capital tidin's indeed. Tell me more. It might be a golden chance to fatten my purse that has grown lean of late.'

'He is renting a rig and driver. Both men will be armed, I might add.'

Frowning slightly, Hal listened to the pair discuss the coming robbery. He concentrated on his breakfast as he feigned indifference to their plans.

'Will you join us, Hal?' Falmouth asked the youngster eventually.

Hal shrugged as he reached for the coffee-pot. 'Why not? It sounds a straightforward piece of banditry.' The mugs on the breakfast tray began to rattle as the table shook slightly. 'What the. . . ?'

Faintly the sound of distant thunder penetrated the room. All three were staring at the mugs as they danced a little jig on top of the tray.

'What the hell . . . is it an earthquake?'

3

Oil lamps were lit in the Big G living-quarters as the darkness closed down over the land. Members of the Grant family were gathered in the dining-room. Extra candles were lit in the room for this was a special evening. The room looked as if it had been decked out for some sort of celebration. On the dresser was a pile of gaily wrapped packages.

Harry Grant stood by the big stone fireplace and built a cigarette. He had a square blunt face that most folk would have considered handsome. A broken nose and a few scars on his face enhanced rather than detracted from his rugged appearance. Though middle-aged he still retained the powerful shoulders of a wrangler.

Sitting in one of the two rockers that stood each side of the fireplace was his wife Allison. She was only a few years younger than her husband. They had two grown-up sons between them. She raised her head to look at the tall grandfather clock standing against the far wall. Carefully groomed, long red hair framed an uncommonly attractive face.

Her youngest son, John Grant lounged in his chair

playing poker. John, in his mid-teens, had his father's square handsome features and showed promise of his breadth of shoulders. The man opposite him was Luke Parsons, Allison Grant's brother and foreman of the Big G cattle ranch.

A chubby, handsome-looking, young black woman came into the room without knocking.

'Ma'am, when is that Hal gonna come home? I cain't keep that turkey dinna in the oven all night. You wan' this here cook to serve you all incinerated blacken' turkey tonight.'

Allison burst out laughing. 'Oh, Melissa, you do take the biscuit for the quaint things you come out with. I should keep a book with all your sayings.'

'I don't care what you keep a book for if'n you were to keep that young Hal on time for his meals.'

Before Allison could answer, hoofbeats could be heard in the yard outside. Everyone looked up expectantly.

'I guess that'll be Hal now, Melissa. You can get ready to serve.'

'If'n he were my son, I'd beat the livin' daylights outa him. He wouldn't be late no more if'n he felt my hand across his backside a time or two.'

Before she could continue, Hal Grant burst into the room.

'Howdy, everyone. Ah, Melissa.' He grabbed the cook and waltzed around the room with her. 'I sure smell something good cooking. What you got for us tonight – burnt sowbelly an' dried out beans?'

The room became alive as Hal cavorted around the furniture whirling the giggling woman in a lively dance.

'Master Hal, you put me down at once. You all make me all dizzy with this here nonsense.'

'Why, Melissa, you're the best dancer in the whole state. You're as light as a feather on them there dancin' feet. You could be an angel swingin' for St Peter. Hallelujah! Hallelujah!'

'Hal,' his mother called, trying unsuccessfully to look severe, 'supper's late as it is. Let Melissa get on with serving.'

Hal finally let Melissa go and she ran giggling from the room.

'Pa.' Hal nodded to his father standing by the fire. 'Ma.' He leaned over Allison and buried his face in her hair. 'You must be the purtiest ma in all the state.'

'Hal, you go an' get ready for supper. You know it's your birthday supper. We all been waiting for you.'

'OK, Ma, I'll have a quick wash in the kitchen sink.'

Before she could say anything more Hal disappeared after Melissa. His family heard a screech and a loud cackling from the region of the kitchen. Harry Grant shook his head in mild despair.

'Did I raise a clown or a son?'

When Hal finally returned from his ablutions the family members gathered round the dining-table and awaited the delivery of the meal.

The main topic of conversation during supper was the stampede.

'Were you in town, Hal, when it went through?' John asked his older brother.

'Sure was.' Hal shook his head in remembrance. 'Never saw anythin' like it. You know when you see a flow of ants goin' hell for lick – well, it were like that only

17

much faster and harder. Nothin' woulda stopped them critters. They poured through Lourdes like a stream of lava. Took out porches, flattened a few wagons an' rigs. Coulda bin worse only horses bolted afore the herd came through. They knew what was comin' all right. Lucky no one was hurt. Kids were in school so they were safe.'

'Jeez,' John breathed, 'Sure wish I'd bin there to see that. Musta bin some sight.'

'Where'd they end up anyways?' Hal asked, as he helped himself to more potatoes and turkey. 'Pass the gravy, Uncle Luke.'

'Pa reckons they're scattered across our range. Gonna be a helluva job to sort them out.'

'John, please try to moderate your language when you're indoors.'

'Sorry, Ma. Anyone know who owns the herd?'

'Ted Partinger rode by during the day an' said as how a bunch of hellraisers came on after the herd and stopped for a drink at the Hot Spur. They kicked the shit – sorry Ma – outa Bill Gristy—'

'Gristy!' Hal interrupted his brother. 'How many of them were there?'

'Ted says no more'n a dozen but only one took on Gristy. Smashed a glass in his face an' then kicked the livin' daylights outa him. Said as his name was Harrison Percy, an' he didn't give a tinker's damn who Gristy was. Then rode outa town, cool as you like.'

Hal was staring at his brother across the table. 'He downed Bill Gristy? Sure must be some tough *hombre*.'

'Anyway Pa says as we've gotta go out tomorrow an' help separate those steers from ourn—'

'Yeah, gonna take some sortin'. But we gotta be out

there in case those rannies decide to separate a few Big G steers along with their own—'

'That's enough gossip,' Allison interrupted. 'This is a special day for our son. You men can talk ranch business another day.' She stood up and went to the doorway. 'Melissa, are you ready?'

The family could not see Melissa's face behind the candle-lit birthday cake as she triumphantly carried it through the doorway.

'Wow! Look at that!'

As they sat around packing away giant slices of sponge cake and icing Allison clapped her hands for attention.

'I guess you can open your presents, Hal.'

Hal grinned over at his mother, traces of icing on his face. 'Best birthday I ever had Ma. You sure bake a mean birthday cake.'

The wrapped presents were on a small table by the fireplace. Hal picked one up. 'From Uncle Luke.' He tore the paper wrapping. His eyes lit up with pleasure. 'A Bowie knife.' He pulled the long blade from the scabbard and made a few swipes in the air. 'Thanks, Uncle Luke.'

Several presents later, a bulky parcel still remained. Hal used the Bowie to cut the string. As the wrapping fell away he reached both hands and slowly picked up a leather gun rig. Nestling in the holster was a pearl-handled Navy Colt.

A reverent look on his face, Hal stroked the outfit. He looked across at Harry Grant standing with his arm around his wife. 'Pa, this is so . . . so . . .' He paused, lost for words. 'I . . . I . . .'

'It's all right, son,' Harry assured him and grinned

19

down at a smiling Allison. 'Had to fight your ma afore she'd 'low me to git it for you. But you're a man now. Try an' act responsible. Eighteen's a good age to be, but it brings duties an' actin' like a man . . . an' . . . an' . . .' Now it was the older man struggling for words. His wife came to the rescue.

'Let's have a tune,' she said, into the embarrassed silence that was growing between father and son and went over to the old piano that had belonged to Harry's mother and lifted the lid.

That night as they undressed in the bedroom, Allison smiled across at her husband.

'Harry, don't judge Hal too harshly. He's still just a kid in spite of turning eighteen.'

Harry removed his shirt. He kept his front to her when he could. No matter how she reassured him he still felt ashamed of the vicious scars across his back. He had acquired them before they were married during a spell in the state penitentiary when falsely accused of murder.

'Allison, when I were eighteen I virtually ran this ranch—'

A finger on his lips stopped him. 'You know, Harry Grant, you sound like a grumpy old man.'

'Hell, Allison. He hangs round with a crowd of low life down at the Mule's Head. Gawd knows what he gits up to. It's a bawdy house, a gambling den an' a drinking hole. Jem Pettifer, the bank manager tole me as how the worst of them down there is a no-good scrounger called Falmouth. Owes money to about everybody in town. Had the gall to tap him for a loan. Pettifer sent him off with a flea in his ear. Tole him he was a disgrace to the community. Didn't mince his words none.'

'Harry, Harry, he'll grow out of it. You'll see. All young men sow their wild oats. In spite of what you say I'm sure you were no angel at that age.'

'That Percy fella that downed Gristy – now there's a man an' a half. Accordin' to Ted he was no more'n a kid himself an' yet he took on Bill Gristy. If'n I had a son like that I'd sure be mighty proud.'

'Harry Grant, that's a terrible thing to say.'

'Humph . . .' Harry snorted as he climbed between the sheets.

Allison stood beside the bed with her fists resting on her hips. Harry stared up at her. In the candlelight she looked just like a girl. His heart tugged within him. She had been no more than a kid when he had first met her and she didn't seem to have changed much in the intervening years.

'Allison,' he said with a catch in his voice, 'you sure are the purtiest woman I ever did see in my whole life.'

'Oh, Harry, you big, adorable man . . .'

Her soft lips meeting his stopped any more conversation. Harry groaned and fell back in the bed. He grabbed his wife and pulled her on top of him. Her body writhed against his and he was instantly aroused.

4

The two men in the carriage seemed in no hurry as they trotted along the highway. The driver was dressed in rough denims and work shirt. A holstered six-shooter could be seen beneath his thick woollen coat. Slotted into pegs in the running board was a shotgun.

The one significant feature that set this man apart from his companion and indeed other fellow creatures was his extraordinary nose. The same colour and texture as a strawberry, it almost glowed in the bright sunlight. One couldn't help wondering if the sun were to go down, whether the gleam from this magnificent snout would be sufficient to guide the gig through the darkness.

His passenger wore a dark suit that had seen better days. A heavy untrimmed moustache covered his upper lip and most of his mouth. He sat as far apart from the red-nosed man as he could as if he were afraid the crimson growth was contagious. His eyes were ever alert and constantly searched the terrain. From time to time he turned and looked over their back trail.

Unlike the moustachioed man, strawberry nose was

seemingly indifferent to his surroundings. He looked as if he was almost asleep as he sat holding the reins. The horses seemed equally apathetic as they plodded along patiently.

Part of the trail wound through a wooded valley. Dipping down into this area the buggy maintained its steady pace. Then up ahead the moustachioed man spied something lying in the trail.

'What'n hell is that up yonder?'

Hal signalled to his brother and John eased his horse away from the other ranch hands. Hal had enlisted his help in some prank he wanted to pull off and John was willing enough to go along with the scheme. The brothers rode towards a clump of trees.

The cowhands in the working group took no notice of the brothers' departure. They were too busy sorting out cattle. The stampede had scattered cattle all over the range and, as Harry Grant had said, it was going to take a lot of hard work to separate the Big G stock.

Once in the cover of the trees, Hal retrieved a roll tied to the back of his saddle. He shook out two long duster coats.

'Put this on,' he ordered John. 'Make sure it covers up everythin'. Button it right up to the neck.'

Dressed in their new attire the brothers took off across country – riding hard.

No Account lay face down in the dust and cursed fervently. He cursed in a low voice for he did not want anyone to hear him. Falmouth had told him of the plan and it had seemed foolproof.

'No Account, you must be the decoy,' Jack Falmouth had said.

'I can decoy right good,' No Account had answered confidently. He was called No Account as that was what his former master used to call him as he whipped him.

He had ended up in Lourdes and found employment at the Mule's Head. As well as swamping, he frequently took part in Jack Falmouth's shady deals. Which was how he found himself lying on the trail cursing at the stationary buggy that had been driven up by another of the gang – the cherry-nosed Bardot.

'Looks like someone in trouble. Mebbe took a tumble from his horse,' Bardot said, to his nervous passenger.

'Loosen up that shotgun,' the man replied. 'I don't like the smell o' this.' Unconsciously he touched his money belt.

'Cain't just leave a fella lyin' on the trail,' Bardot insisted. 'I couldn't live with m'self to just drive on by.'

'Take it up easy, an' git out that shotgun.'

Bardot obediently dislodged the weapon and laid it across his knees. He started the team forward again. Once the buggy was near enough Bardot hauled on the reins.

'Better see what gives,' he commented 'Best get down and have a look.'

His companion was nervously watching the trees bordering the trail. As Bardot stepped to the ground several things happened at once.

A tree suddenly leaned over and crashed to the trail narrowly missing No Account and effectively blocking the way forward. No Account screamed as a branch from the falling tree whipped across his head and gave him a nasty fright. He jumped to his feet and began firing his revolver into the trees. Bardot clambered back into the gig and sat with his hands in the air. Two masked men appeared suddenly at the roadside with levelled pistols.

'OK, fellas, git your hands up, pronto. This is a hold-up.'

The one who spoke looked broad and overblown. He seemed to wheeze rather than breathe as if he had been running all the way from Lourdes. The men in the buggy slowly raised their hands.

'Throw down your money.'

'Money? I ain't got no money,' Bardot whined.

By now No Account had reloaded and startled everyone by commencing to fire off shots once more into the trees. The fat man waddled across and whacked the Negro on the back of the head with his pistol.

'Fer Gawd's sake, stop that shootin'. The whole county'll be about our ears.'

'Gawddamn your white trash ass, what in tarnation you have to do that fer?' No Account wailed. 'I oughta shoot your fat, white ass.'

This altercation gave the passenger in the buggy a chance to go for his gun. As he struggled to extract his pistol from its holster, Bardot threw his arms around him.

'Please, mister, don't do that. Don't give them badmen excuse to shoot us,' he pleaded as he wrestled with his companion. The nearness of the bulbous nose caused the man to rear back in alarm.

'Gawddamn it, let me go, you gawddamn coward. I'll show these bastards not to mess with Griff Tracey.'

The two men wrestled in the buggy seat with Bardot attempting to keep the victim both safe and harmless. His passenger was at a severe disadvantage. It was clear he was labouring under a double dilemma. Occupied with the necessity of unlimbering his gun and trying to shake loose from the driver it was obvious he was terrified of coming into contact with Bardot's repulsive nose. His dilemma was solved when the fat outlaw shoved his revolver into his midriff.

'Stop that foolin' around an' hand over that money belt.'

It was a hopeless situation for the hapless man. All three of the bandits now covered him with their guns and he had no chance of reaching his own weapon while his driver clung to him so passionately.

'Gawddamn your hides, I'll see you all swing for this,' Tracey blustered. 'The law'll hunt you down and hang everyone of you.'

'Just throw down that there money an' you can go on your way,' the fat outlaw instructed. 'Otherwise I'll blow a hole in your guts an' leave you out here for the buzzards.'

'Git your damned hands off'n me,' Tracey swore at his driver. 'How am I suppose to do anythin' with you clung to me like a plague?'

Reluctantly, Bardot released his passenger. 'I were only tryin' to save your life, Mr Tracey. These fellas are sure bad'uns. They'd'a shot us both for sure. Nobody'd thank me for bringin' back a corpse in this here buggy.'

It did not take many minutes for the outlaws to relieve Griff Tracey of his money belt. They disappeared into the trees leaving a fuming Tracey calling curses after them.

'Git back to town,' he snarled at his buggy driver. 'I'm gonna post a reward for them bastards. Cain't be hard to catch a fat man and a half-wit Nigra an' the other fella. How in the hell'd they know I had that money belt?'

While he fumed, Bardot was turning the buggy around and was soon taking his disgruntled passenger back to Lourdes.

'You sure this is where you tied them thar horses, Pike?'

Inside the cover of the trees the bandits had pulled down their bandannas revealing the features of Falmouth, No Account and Pike – a shifty looking half-breed with only one eye.

'Sure. Me sure it here.'

The bandits looked around anxiously. There was no sign of the three horses that were their means of transport to and from the scene of the robbery.

'I've a notion to blow a hole in that thick head of yourn, yuh half-wit 'breed.' Falmouth looked around in despair. 'How'n hell we gonna git back to town? If'n we don't git outa here pronto there'll be a posse here ready to hang us from them thar trees.' It was as he said the last words he saw the two riders sitting silently watching them.

They wore buttoned up dusters. Ominously they also had gunnysacks pulled over their faces. Holes for mouth and eyes had been crudely cut in the material giving the figures a menacing and devilish appearance. More threatening still were the Colts pointing steadily at the trio of bandits.

'Lord'a'mercy,' No Account screeched and dropped to his knees. 'Lord'a'mercy . . . it weren't me . . . massa. It weren't me. I's innocent. I swear on my mutha's grave.'

He lapsed into incoherent babbling.

'That there money belt, fat man,' a disembodied voice called out, 'just bring it over here. An' be mighty careful where you put your hands. Anyone touches an iron and there's three dead men we'll save the county the expense of hangin'.'

Falmouth was shaking so much his teeth rattled. 'Don' shoot, mister. You can have the money. Please don' shoot.'

'Just do as you're told an' bring that money here.'

As Falmouth hurried to hand over the money belt he was trembling so much the coins could be heard jingling together. The sinister figure in the gunnysack mask took the belt and tucked it into his saddle-bag.

'Should we just shoot them rodents for the hell of it, Jesse?' the second figure queried.

'Jesse! You ain't the James brothers, are you?' Tears trembled on fat cheeks. 'Look, mister, you ain't got no cause to shoot us. We ain't done no one no harm. We's just hold-up men tryin' to make a honest livin',' Fralmouth pleaded.

'Hell, Frank, they's recognized us. Guess there's nothing else fer it. Cain't leave them to raise hue an' cry after us. Tell you what, fatso, I'll give you fair chance. I'll turn my horse round an' tuck my iron away. You three all turn round an' when Frank here gives the signal you all go for your irons. Frank'll stay out of it. Just me agin you three. Seem fair to you?'

Falmouth could only shake his head helplessly. 'Please, Mr Jesse, I won't tell no one. Just let us go. You . . . you could kill No Account and this 'breed but just spare me.'

'Turn around!' The order was barked out suddenly. Weeping helplessly, Falmouth turned around, as did his 'breed accomplice. No Account shuffled around on his knees and prayed with his eyes tightly closed.

'Just let me git this here horse turned about'

The sound of horses moving in the trees intruded on the senses of the terrified Falmouth. The silence pressed down as he waited for the dread word from the notorious James brothers. And waited. And waited.

5

'You wanna come into town and see the fun?'

Hal grinned across at his brother. They had discarded the dusters and now wore their normal range gear.

'You bet,' John said enthusiastically, then frowned as a thought struck him. 'What about the money belt, what you gonna do with that?'

'Take it to Sheriff Blunt. We tell him we found it. It has the poor man's name on it. He'll git it back.'

'Right,' yelled John. 'Race you to town. Last one in buys the drinks.' He spurred his horse catching Hal by surprise.

'You're too young to drink,' Hal yelled after his brother, as he urged his own mount into a gallop.

The brothers were established in the Mule's Head, long before Falmouth and his gang returned. The hold-up men were dusty and weary. It had been an exhausting search for their mounts – hidden by Hal and his brother while the bandits were busy staging their hold-up.

'Oh, Hal, Hal, I wish you'd been there,' called Falmouth on spying Hal and his brother at one of the tables. 'Drink, drink, let me have a drink before I expire.'

He sat heavily beside the brothers and downed Hal's glass of whiskey without asking permission. Hal grinned at John.

'What in tarnation's the matter, Jack? You look like you've fought off a pack of wild dogs.'

'Oh, Hal, you don't know the half of it.' He picked up John's drink and downed that also.

At that moment Bardot came in – spied Falmouth and came across eagerly.

'Jack, my man, where have you hidden the goods?' He leered heavily at the brothers.

John shifted his chair back to put more distance between himself and the fearsome nose. Falmouth looked pained then buried his head in his hands.

'Gawddamn it, if ever there was a man born to misfortune it were me.'

'What's the matter, Jack?' Hal asked. 'John, go an' order a bottle. Fat Jack looks wore out.'

'But ... but ... I don't wanna miss anythin',' protested John.

'Don't worry. Nothin's gonna spill till you git that there bottle,' Hal assured his brother.

When the whiskey was duly delivered, Hal continued with his interrogation of the fat man.

'Now, Jack, tell us what the fuss is about.' As he spoke Hal poured generous measures for all.

'Fuss! I'll tell you what fuss. We was robbed,' the fat man replied. Grabbing his glass he emptied it in one gulp.

'We was robbed.' He held his glass out for a refill but Hal ignored it.

'What you talkin' about, you fat fool? You set out to do

31

a robbery an' you was robbed!'

'Yes, Hal, we was robbed!' In desperation Falmouth made a grab for the bottle, but Hal pulled it back out of his reach.

'Jack, no more drink. You've bin drinkin' too much already to tell a tale like that. Robbed! What the hell ya talkin' about?'

'Oh, Jack,' wailed Bardot, momentarily taking his finger from inside his strawberry nose and blinking in distress at his companion in crime.

The fat man glanced around then lowered his voice as if afraid of being overheard. 'We did the job slick as a whistle. When we got back to the horses these here fellas was lyin' in wait fer us.'

'Fellas, Jack! How many?' asked Hal.

Thick lips twisted as the fat man thought about the answer. 'Musta bin twenty or thirty. Hidin' in the trees they was . . .'

'What'd you do, Jack?' Hal interrupted. 'Twenty or thirty desperadoes was a mite too many even fer you.'

'What'd I do, Hal? I tell you what I did. I went for my iron. No robbin' sons of bitches was gonna take my hard-earned money, no sirree. I emptied my Colt into those hardcases. Musta killed five or six of them. Lead was flyin' in those trees like it were a snowstorm. No Account was blazin' away by me an' so was Pike. Then Hal, I could see it were hopeless. There were just too many of those galoots. Then they called out they was . . .' The fat man closed his eyes and shook his head in despair. 'They tole us they was the James gang.' Falmouth paused for effect.

'What!' Hal's eyes were wide with disbelief.

'I knew there was no hope for us. But I didn't give in

easy. No sirree – not Jack Falmouth. I struck a deal. I tole them to spare my companions and fer me an' Jesse to have it out man to man – just him an' me.'

At this juncture, John Grant snorted and grabbed for his bandanna. He coughed violently for some moments before surfacing again with red face and watering eyes.

'Sorry about that,' Hal apologized. 'He's not used to strong drink.'

The fat man held out his glass and Hal refilled it.

'What, Jack, you up agin Jesse James? Gawddamn it, Jack, no one goes up agin Jesse James.'

'Hal, he chickened out. Said as he wouldn't go up agin the likes of Jack Falmouth. So I says if'n he let my men live I'd give him the money. But Jesse wouldn't come outa hidin'. No sir, he sent one of his men to pick up the money. Then they all rode off – the whole pack of them. Musta bin forty or fifty of them there James boys – forty or fifty.'

'What about the ones you killed, Jack? Shouldn't someone collect them? Might be a reward fer them there outlaws – dead or alive it mostly is.'

'What?' The fat man looked startled for a moment. 'Naw, Hal, they took their dead 'uns with them. Packed them outa there on their own horses.'

Hal suddenly frowned and looked hard at the fat outlaw. 'Were these James boys wearing dusters an' black hats?'

'That's right, Hal . . . dusters an' black hats.'

'All fifty of them, Jack, all wearing dusters?'

'That's right, Hal, might have bin mor'n fifty. With all that lead flying I wasn't payin' too much 'tention to numbers.'

Hal was looking thoughtful. 'Was this by any chance out by Preachers Wood?'

'Yeah, Hal, that's the place. We hid in the woods fer Bardot to bring the gent to us so's we could rob him.'

'Fifty you say?'

'Mebbe more, I was too fired up to take proper notice. I just wanted to kill those sons of bitches.'

'John, was that where we saw them two riders coming from?'

'Sure, Hal, when we heard the shootin' we rode over a piece and saw these two fellas in dusters. They was ridin' away from Preachers Wood—' John broke off. 'You don't reckon they was the James boys we saw? Gawdamighty!'

The brothers stared at Falmouth. The fat man looked from one to the other of the Grants. 'What you sayin', boys? You tryin' to say you saw the James boys ridin' outa there?'

'More than fifty, you reckon, Jack?' Hal was remorseless in his grilling.

'Hal, there was so much firin' goin' on . . . it sure sounded like twenty or so.'

'Twenty now, not fifty or sixty?'

'Hal, Hal, when bullets are flyin' you don't take much account of anythin' else. I was too busy shootin'. I didn't have time to count.'

'But we saw two, Jack. Just two riders came outa that wood. What about the ones you killed? You say they took the bodies with them. We didn't see no bodies on no horses.'

'Gawddamn it, Hal, let's have another drink 'fore I collapse of thirst.' Falmouth poured another glass of whiskey. Suddenly his eyes brightened. 'That's right, they said as they would leave in ones an' twos. Didn't want to attract attention – whole group of them ridin' round the country.'

It was too much for John. His snorting became uncontrollable. Hal looked at his brother – head buried in his hands, shoulders shaking uncontrollably – and he broke down too.

Falmouth stared at the brothers rolling about in the chairs helpless with mirth. He took the opportunity to pour another drink and went back to contemplating the strange behaviour of the Grants.

'Gawddamn sons of bitches,' he muttered, and while the brothers rolled about in their chairs hooting with laughter he occupied himself with the serious business of emptying the whiskey bottle while they were so distracted.

6

'Git your backsides into that herd. This ain't no Sunday outin'. Gawddamn it, try an' earn the money I pay you, you lazy good fer nothings.'

It was hard work and no one worked harder than the boss of the Big G. His hands didn't mind him shouting at them. He never asked them to do anything he wouldn't do himself.

Harry Grant was in the midst of the steers working his pony as hard as he worked himself. He was using his coiled lariat to slap recalcitrant steers into doing what he wanted them to do. The cattle bellowed and thrashed around churning up the ground.

A belligerent steer made a short charge at the big man and his pony. Harry yelled at the beast and using only his knees manoeuvred the pony out of range of the wicked horns. At the same time he managed to slash the rebellious steer across the rump with his rope. It plunged back into the herd and horse and rider continued the thankless task of separating out Big G cattle from the stock that had so abruptly invaded the home pastures.

Harry, along with his cowhands, was tired and dusty

from the continuous effort of the unremitting work. Once a bunch of steers had been cut out from the mess of cattle they had to be herded back to a clear part of the range. The work took its toll of men and horses. Exhausted men made mistakes and already Harry was two hands down from injury and a cow pony had gone lame and had to be replaced. Harry swore long and luridly and plunged back into the mêlée.

His foreman and brother-in-law, Luke Parsons was in charge of the separated cattle. He and a team of three cowboys were herding the segregated steers to a holding ground well away from the polluted area. One thing puzzled Harry. There was no sign of the men who had ridden in after the runaway herd.

His crew had been at the exhausting work since sun-up and now the same sun was working towards the opposite horizon. Harry rose in his stirrups and waved his arm in a high arc. He kept waving till he saw the work crew reining in and looking in his direction. When he had their attention he signalled them to finish up. They'd worked hard that day and indeed the last two days.

'Tell Luke I'll be along a bit later,' he instructed one of the hands.

'You gonna carry on workin', boss?'

'No. Bin seein' some smoke back towards the creek. I wanna see what's causin' it. I've a feelin' it might be the owners of them there steers we bin chasin' around for the last couple days. Tell Luke I'll be back 'fore supper.'

He followed the smoke signs and, as he drew closer, he could see some activity in the basin of the creek. A wagon was parked beneath a big spreading tree and tents were pitched nearby. The smell of cooking wafted up to the rancher. It made him realize he was hungry. He angled the pony on down towards the camp.

The man who had been bending over the cook fire straightened as Harry Grant rode up.

'Howdy, stranger. I guess you smelt m' cuisine from over yonder hill an' wondered if'n you had wandered into the Garden of Eden.'

Harry laughed. The man wore an apron and had a grizzled beard.

'Guess you're right at that. Sure smells good.'

'If'n you want coffee, it's hot. Supper will be ready when the boys git back'

Harry climbed from his mount and helped himself to a mug of coffee. While he drank he built a smoke and examined the camp. He noted the firewood piled high. Items of men's laundry hung on a makeshift line. The tents he had already seen from afar. A corral had been fashioned from trimmed tree trunks.

He settled himself on a log. A series of these temporary seats were arranged around the camp-fire.

The cooking place had a look of permanence about it being constructed with rocks and chinked with mud daubs. An iron grid lay across the top and several steaks were laid on this in the process of being grilled. The grease from the meat dripped on to the flames and hissed and spat continuously. A frying pan was filled with partly baked biscuits while a large pot of beans was positioned to one side.

'Bin here long?'

'Coupla days.' The cook moved pots and steaks dextrously around on the fire. He moved the grid to one side and fed the fire with fresh logs.

Further conversation was interrupted by the clatter of an approaching wagon. Several riders came into view behind the vehicle. It was piled high with fresh-sawn logs. More riders came in from across the creek. They whooped and yelled in high spirits as they arrived and joshed the cook who cursed them with evident good humour. Harry was greeted with nods and 'Howdys' as the crew dismounted and gathered round the cook fire.

Two men rode out of the trees. Harry recognized one of them as the young hellion Ted Partinger said had floored Bill Gristy. Ted's description fitted the bearded youngster. The other man was older – a weather-beaten man with a drooping, grey-speckled moustache. The men dismounted, turned their horses into the corral and came on over to the cook fire.

'Howdy, stranger. You passing thro' or stayin' for supper? We ain't hirin' at the moment if'n that's what you're after.' The younger of the two spoke. He had a close cropped reddish beard. On nearer inspection Harry realized the beard made him look older than he was.

'I could ask you the same question – you just passin' through or stayin'?'

'Come an' git it!' The cook yelled out his invitation at the top of his voice even though the hands were gathered close around the fire. Things got a bit noisy as the cowhands lined up for grub.

The young man poured himself a coffee before turning to the big rancher. His eyes were unfriendly as he looked at Harry. 'What's it to yuh, fella?'

'I take it those cattle that run wild through the place belong to you?' Harry asked, answering the young man's question with a question of his own.

'I said, what's it to yuh?'

'If'n those cattle aren't yourn then we'll just have to round them up and put our brand on them.'

'You put a brandin' iron on any of our cattle and we'll hang you for rustlin',' the older man spoke.

'So they are your cattle. Then why aren't you roundin' them up?'

The younger man had sauntered over to where Harry sat.

'You've a big mouth, mister. Now finish your coffee and git outa here afore someone kicks your butt.'

Harry poured the dregs of coffee on to the ground and stood up. 'This happens to be private range. It belongs to the Big G. You're welcome to stay a few days but I'd take it kindly if'n you and your outfit took your herd and moved on. There ain't room for two herds on this range.'

'Son of a bitch, no one tells me what to do.'

The red-bearded youngster moved to confront Harry. He noted the youngster was almost as tall as he was himself.

Maybe because the account of the beer glass in Bill Gristy's face was fresh in his mind, the rancher moved so fast. As the mug of hot coffee came up Harry grabbed the youth's wrist. At the same time he smashed his big fist into the red beard. Once, twice, three times. The man crashed back and tumbled over a log seat.

Even as the older Percy went for his gun, he found himself staring down the barrel of a Colt that seemed to jump into the big rancher's hand. Harry cocked the Colt. Tom Percy licked his lips and kept his hand where it was.

'There's a dozen or more of us, mister. You'll be dead

afore you pull that trigger.'

'I'll be takin' six with me if that's the case, an' your name is on the first bullet.'

The chatter by the cooking fire had stilled.

'Say the word, boss. We'll kill the son of a bitch.'

Suddenly Harry reached down and hauled the groaning Harrison Percy to his feet. It was a tribute to his great strength of arm that he did this while holding the Colt steady on the senior member of the Percy family. He pulled the youngster close.

'I came here to see if'n you rannies needed any help gittin' your herd together. I see you have no intention of movin' on. If'n you think to settle here let me tell you again: this is private land – Big G range. My name is Harry Grant. I own the Big G. I'm givin' you notice: be off my land before the end of the next week. It'll take you that long to git your herd together. If you're not off my land by the deadline, I'll drive you off with or without your herd.'

Slowly he backed away from the watching men.

'Me an' your friend here is takin' a little ride. You make any unfriendly move agin me an' he'll end up with a hole in his head.'

Reaching his mount Harry reached up and removed his rope. Quickly he looped it around the dazed man's neck then swung into the saddle.

'Hup there, boy,' he urged the horse.

As they went forward Harry kept his gun trained on the men around the camp-fire.

'Remember what I said: I'll give you a week at most.'
All the time Harry was drawing further and further from the camp.

'You're a dead man, Grant. You an' yoor family. When we've finished with you we'll dig up the graves of your ancestors and scatter their bones over this here range. No one messes with the Percy family an' lives to tell the tale. You're dead!'

His captive stumbled and went down on his knees. Harry loosened the noose and pulled the lariat free. He thumbed a couple of shots over the heads of the watching men. As they scrambled for cover he hit his heels into his mount.

'Hup boy, go . . . go!' he yelled, and the horse lit out at a dead run.

Gradually as he raced into the gathering darkness the shots fired in his direction faded into the distance.

Harry cursed as he rode. He had hoped to make a peaceful incursion into the camp but the newcomers obviously did not take kindly to being ordered about. They looked a tough bunch. But they had to be moved on, otherwise they were taking over part of Big G range. They had to be stopped now. The felled logs the work team had dragged to the campsite didn't look like firewood. The looked suspiciously like timber cut for building.

Harry eased up his mount's headlong run and settled into a gentle lope. He reckoned he would still be in time for supper.

7

Wagons rolling through Lourdes were not an unusual sight. Hal Grant would not have taken much notice of the covered wagon only for the fact that he nearly walked out in front of it.

He had been mulling over the prank he had played on Jack Falmouth. The fat man's boasting of his imagined exploits against the James gang had kept his brother John and himself in high amusement. Hal had only to broach the subject and Falmouth would launch into his fantasy world where famous bandits trembled at the mere mention of his name.

'Tell me again how you faced down Jesse James. You know, Jack, my blood runs cold to think you was that close to death.'

'Close to death, hell. It were them there James boys that was close to death. I reckon I winged that there Jesse an' that's why he were afraid to face me. Soon takes the starch out of a fella if he has one of Jack Falmouth's slugs in him.'

Each telling of the tale became more and more imaginative. There were hundreds of the James gang swarm-

ing about in the battle of Parson Woods. But Fearless
Jack Falmouth fought them to a standstill.

More and more of the outlaws died with each
retelling. The episode began to take on the scale of a
skirmish on the battlefields of the recent War Between
the States.

The air cracked above Hal Grant's hat and he instinc-
tively ducked. His hand involuntary went to the butt of
his newly acquired Colt. Then he back stepped smartly as
a bullock tried to trample him underfoot.

'Gawddamn half-wits walkin' out in the road. Careful
where you're steppin', dungbrains.'

Recovering his wits, Hal stood and glared in anger at
the figure standing on the driving step of the big covered
wagon. An angry retort was on his lips when something
stopped him. That something was the realization that the
driver yelling at him was a young woman.

A battered hat was pulled down over long black hair
that had been tied back with a leather thong. Beneath
the hat brim, deep-set dark eyes glared out at him with
sparks of anger in them. A long, slim, straight nose flared
with annoyance. Red, full lips pouted angrily.

His own mouth fell open in admiration and he did
indeed stare like a half-wit at the female bullwhacker.
The wagon had stopped beside Hal and frowning eyes
glared down at him.

'I take it you're the town idiot. Sure hope it gits better
after this.'

The bullwhip cracked again in the air.

'Hip! Hip!'

The oxen leaned into the traces and the wagon rolled
forward leaving Hal in the middle of the road feeling

extremely foolish.

'I . . . I . . .' His mouth opened and closed in imitation of a fish taken from a lake, but he could think of nothing to say. Then it was too late and he was staring at the rear of the wagon. He continued across the road and, vastly intrigued by his encounter, followed the wagon.

The large vehicle lumbered down the main street of Lourdes leaving fresh ruts in its wake. He had to admit the girl knew how to handle the team of oxen. She had managed to crack her whip over his hat and at the same time bring the team of lumbering beasts to a halt before it could run him down. He grinned ruefully as he recalled her insults.

The outfit pulled up before the Hot Spur saloon. Hal quickened his step. He wanted another chance to examine the tomboy driver.

The slim figure of the girl jumped lightly to the ground in front of the saloon and stood hands on hips. Slowly she coiled her bullwhip as she gazed up at the lurid signs that advertised the establishment's various attractions. She stepped forward and entered the saloon. Hal followed quickly. He wanted a close-up of the fiery vixen.

As he walked up the boardwalk he was almost knocked down by a man hurrying out of the saloon and running down the street. Hal staggered back against the wall of the Hot Spur and glared after the man.

'Gawddamn it, have I become invisible today?' he growled indignantly to no one in particular. Then he slipped inside the batwing doors.

There was a dearth of customers in the saloon this early in the morning. What few there was were staring towards the bar. Hal saw the female bullwhacker in conversation with the barkeep. He sauntered up to stand near the pair. The barkeep was searching in his ear with a spent match.

'A herd you say, came through in the last week or so? Reckon we did see them thar cows. Came right plumb smack through the town. Didn't stop for nothin' like. They was runnin' so hard they almost took the town with 'em.'

'What do you mean runnin'? Weren't there no one with them – like cowboys?'

'Nope! No cowboys with them thar cows. They was runnin' on their own. Runnin' like somethin' spooked 'em.'

The conversation was going round in circles. Hal decided he could try to help.

'Pardon me, miss, can I be of any assistance?'

Inky pools of witchery were turned fully towards him. A sardonic grin twitched across full petulant lips.

'Well, well. If it ain't the village idiot.'

A shock of pure physical magnetism rippled down Hal's spine as he looked into those jet-black eyes. It had the effect of rendering him speechless.

'Even better, a village idiot who speaks one sentence a day.' The girl turned back to the barkeep. 'Listen, mister, are you related to this dumbass idiot? Don't answer that! I guess everyone in this two-bit town is related. I ask a simple question: did a herd – a large herd, pass this way in the last week or so?'

Before the barman could reply the batwings swung in and a group of men entered. At their head was Bill Gristy. Hal stared in fascination at the feared pugilist.

Bandages criss-crossed the man's face effectively disguising his ugly features. Holes had been left for eyes, nose and mouth. Gristy walked up to the bar and stopped beside the girl.

'You askin' 'bout those thar cowboys with the runaway herd?' Gristy's question snapped out like one of his punches.

The girl looked at the bandaged man for a moment before replying. 'Well, well, well. First I meet a walkin' dummy and now there appears a talkin' mummy.'

Hal watching just a few feet away could imagine Gristy's beefy face beneath the bandages becoming suffused with anger.

'Watch that mouth, gal,' he gritted out, 'or it could git you in trouble. I asked a civil question an' I expect a civil answer.'

For a moment Hal suspected the girl was tempted to rile Gristy some more but her need for information overrode her waspish tongue.

'As a matter of fact I was lookin' for some men on a cattle drive. I don't know nothin' about no runaway herd.'

'What's your interest in these fellas, anyways?'

'Mister No Face, can we just cut the crap? My simple question is – did a herd pass this way in the last week or so? That's all I wanna know.'

Suddenly Gristy thrust his bandaged face up close to the girl. 'Listen, you cheap whore, those cowboys did this to my face. They're not leavin' this territory alive. Now if'n you're the camp whore, Bill Gristy says, stay outa Lourdes. When I'm good an' ready I'm comin' for those bastards. Now git that whore-wagon off the street. Your sort's not welcome. We got enough whores.'

Hal was appalled at the saloon owner's behaviour. He stepped up to the pair still glaring at each other, eyeball to eyeball.

'Hang on there, Gristy, that's no way to talk to a lady.' Slowly the bandaged face turned to Hal. Gristy looked the youngster up and down.

'Don't mess with me, boy. Run back home to your mammy. Your pants need changing.'

Step by step Hal backed away. The anger was growing in him. Not hot anger, but a cold seething rage at this man dismissing him so offhandedly. His arms hung loose by his sides. He was very much aware of the weight of the new Colt against his hip.

'You need to 'pologize, Gristy. Ain't right to insult no stranger comin' into town.

Gristy turned fully round to face Hal. The girl turned around too, her face flushed with anger. Gristy's remarks had been like a slap in the face.

Hal kept his gaze on the holes behind which the pugilist's eyes blazed in anger. For a moment the two men faced each other. Hal, tall and slim, still a youth – not yet grown into the man he would become. Standing before him was the brutal mass of Bill Gristy, his body hardened and muscular, bearing the scars of numerous fights both in and out of the ring.

'Well, well. The puppy dog has a little tin gun an' thinks it makes him a man. You run on home, sonny. This is a man's saloon. Boys shouldn't mix in grown-ups' games. Do you want some milk afore you go?' Gristy half turned to the bar. 'Set up some milk for the whelp, barkeep.'

48

Hal's anger still seethed within him. The scathing remarks stung him. He knew it was foolish even as he did it but then the girl was watching him. Making sure his movements were slow and deliberate he reached down and unbuckled his gunbelt. There was a dull thud as the rig slipped to the sawdust at his feet.

'I need no gun to face a piece of dung like you, Gristy. All you're fit for is insultin' ladies.'

Whatever else Hal had a mind to say never got said for without warning Gristy rushed straight at him. A sledge-hammer hit Hal in the chest and flung him back on to the saloon floor. Gristy, eager to stomp this upstart boy, and with his sight hindered by the bandages, tangled his feet on Hal's discarded weaponry and stumbled forward on to his knees.

Hal, dizzy with excruciating pain in his chest where Gristy's fist had struck, saw the bandaged face kneeling before him and lashed out hard with his boot. The boot heel smashed into Gristy's mouth driving the big man sideways. Hal happened to be wearing his spurs for he had been on his way to the livery. The rowel snagged on the bandages and Hal's foot was dragged after Gristy's face. With a snarl of rage Gristy grabbed the entangled boot and hauled the youngster towards him.

'Son of a bitch, I'm gonna kill you.'

Hal lashed out with his fists but the pugilist ignored the punches. His big scarred hands gripped Hal's shirt and pulled him even closer. Hal tried a head-butt, which got nowhere near its target. Then the pugilist's hands closed on Hal's throat. The big hands almost completely encircled the youngster's neck.

'Start squealin', boy. If'n you beg for mercy I might

just let you live – a little longer.'

The big hands were steel clamps fastened on Hal's neck. He tensed his neck muscles but had no effect on the tightening band that was slowly choking off his air supply. He tried to get his knees up but the weight of the big man was too much. Hal's face was reddening and his mouth gaped open as he tried to suck in air.

'You wet your pants yet, boy?' the bandaged face taunted.

Hal writhed and struggled beneath that choking, terrible grip. He might as well have been trying to move the fully laden wagon parked outside the saloon.

The man was fashioned from granite with a vice-like grip. Hal's eyes were beginning to bulge. His face had turned crimson. The bandaged face hovering above him took on the aspect of a white cloud. Little grey specks floated across the cloud like birds floating on a thermal. He tried to speak but no sound came.

He wanted to curse and swear and call the man a bastard and a son of a bitch. His mouth worked but he had no breath to speak the words. He could feel the pain in his lungs and chest growing till his body seemed to be on fire.

The grey dots floating in the white cloud became black dots and began to merge together. He made one last supreme effort and amazingly the mummy face leaned down and pressed intimately against him. He could feel the cloth of the bandage hard against his nose and mouth. A strange grunt came out of the space that would have been the mouth. The inexorable pressure on his larynx lessened.

Hal desperately sucked in air and a loose piece of

bandage entered his mouth. It did not seem to matter as the life giving air was pumped into his lungs. He tried to spit and breathe at the same time. The mummified face slid to one side taking the loose bandage with it. Hal found himself staring up at the girl who had been the cause of his plight.

'I can tell you an' mummy are real close. Do you wanna git on top now?'

Hal could not speak. He massaged his throat then heaved the weighty mass of the pugilist from him.

'What happened?' he croaked, as he sat up.

The girl showed him the coiled bullwhip and tapped her palm against the thick, leather handle.

'Took a couple of raps but I got through in the end.'

Hal grinned ruefully. 'Looks as if I owe you one.'

She held out a hand and Hal took it gratefully. With surprising strength she heaved him to his feet. They stood like that, hand grasping hand for a few moments, gazing at each other.

'Guess I owe you too. Shall we call it quits?'

' 'Fraid I didn't do much. Shouldn't of took my gun off,' Hal said despondently and bent to pick up his discarded gunbelt.

Gristy's cronies were gathering round their fallen leader. Hal and the girl ignored them and walked out of the saloon. They stood on the boardwalk and regarded each other.

'You were enquirin' 'bout the herd. It went through here a few days ago. The reason the townsfolk were so riled up, the herd stampeded through the town. Did a mite of damage. Then one of your boys did that to Gristy's face. Story goes he smashed a beer glass and cut him real bad.'

'Guy with a red beard – youngish like?' she queried.

'Dunno, didn't see it myself. Said as his name was Harrison Percy.'

'Where are they now? Which direction did they head?'

'Out towards Potter's Creek. Leastaways that's where they were couple of days ago.' Hal did not mention the confrontation his father had with the rogue cowboys. 'What's your interest in them?'

'That red-bearded hothead is my brother. I'm followin' on behind the herd with the family possessions.' The girl indicated the laden wagon. The oxen stood patiently awaiting their mistress. 'What's your name.'

'Hal, my name's Hal.'

Hal deliberately did not give his surname. When she met her brother she would be sure to link Hal Grant with Harry Grant. He did not want her to know his father had a run-in with her family and had ordered them off his land.

'I'm Morgan Percy.' She took his hand and shook it like a man. They grinned at each other and suddenly Hal knew he wanted this girl. It was with utter certainty he knew no other girl would ever satisfy him after meeting her.

She was fiery – she had thumped Bill Gristy over the head in order to rescue him – but most of all she was beautiful. In her dark smouldering way she had burned a brand on Hal Grant's heart.

8

'Morgan, you're a sight for sore eyes,' Tom Percy greeted his daughter, and hugged her hard against him.

Morgan's eyes sparkled as she looked around the encampment. She noted the logs laid out in regular formation indicating the outlines of a dwelling.

'You plannin' on settlin' here, Pa?'

'Well, now,' Tom looked around him while reaching his fingers up under his hat and scratching at his hair, 'guess there's worse places to settle. Got good water, plenty of grass. All the things we've bin scarce of lately. Whaddaya think?'

'Don't nobody own this here land? Seems too good to be true if'n no one has a claim to such prime land.'

'Wa-al, that could be just a mite problematic. We've already had a run-in with the owner of this land or claims he's the owner. Warned us off. Harrison's gone to the next nearest town to send for some help. Figurin' on givin' this Grant fella a whole hassle of trouble. Mebbe leave us alone if'n he thinks we're too tough to take on.' He had led his daughter to the camp-fire. 'Fresh coffee sound good to you?'

'Miss Morgan, I do declare,' the cook greeted the girl with real pleasure. 'You sure brighten up our days. You set yourself down an' I'll fix you somethin' to eat. Biscuits an' molasses an' hot coffee coming up.'

Basking in the warm welcome, Morgan perched on a log and watched as her dad eased himself down beside her.

'This landowner wasn't the only one you riled up, Dad, was it? I met a man in that town. Name of Bill Gristy – had his face all bandaged – like a regular mummy. What happened?'

'Hah!' Tom Percy smacked his hand on his knee. 'That sure do beat all, Morgan. Fella came into the saloon while we was havin' a quiet drink. Tries to push your brother around. Big mistake on his part. Harrison beat him into the sawdust. Left him bleeding on the floor of that there saloon. Reckon he'll think twice afore he tangles with a Percy again.'

'Pa, I met this Gristy. I stopped to ask directions an' he set on me. Young fella came to my rescue. Called this Gristy out.' Her eyes grew slightly moist as she recalled the young man standing alone on the saloon floor taking on the brawler who was bent on insulting her. Suddenly she grinned. 'Had to rescue him from Gristy. Had him on the floor strangulatin' the poor man. So I whopped him a few times with the handle of my ox-popper. Guess he don't have much love for the Percy family.'

'Son'a bitch! You done what? You done whopped that fella with your bullwhip. Ha! Ha! Ha!' Tom Percy slapped his knee in exuberance. 'Wait'll I tell your brother. He's gonna be so proud of his little sister.' And Tom laughed long and rocked back and forth while his daughter smiled fondly on her daddy.

It was late that night when Harrison Percy rode into the camp to be greeted by an ecstatic sister.

'Oh, Harrison, so good to see you.' Brother and sister hugged warmly. 'Where've you bin?'

'Can a man git a mug of coffee and a plate of beans afore he's interrogated?' Harrison complained.

Seated with a plate of biscuits and beans Harrison began to tell his sister of the situation they found themselves in.

'This Grant seems to own most of the land round here. He runs a vast outfit. Its prime cattle country. Waal, he's ordered us of'n his land. Cain't say I blame him. I'd do the same in his place.' Harrison spooned beans down him like a starving man. 'I've wired for the Mortimers to come an' join us. We'll need help, Sis. Things might git rough.'

Morgan stared at her brother. The camp-fire flickered, alternately lighting and throwing into shadow the features of brother and sister.

'It's to be a shootin' war then?'

'That's the way its gotta be, Sis. Grant came in here – put a rope round my neck an' dragged me outa the camp. Then told us we had a week to git off his land. Nobody does that to a Percy an' gits away with it.'

'An' so the Mortimers will ride up here to join you an' Pa.'

Harrison scooped up the last of the beans and dropped the plate at his feet. The silence stretched between them each lost in their own thoughts.

Morgan stared into the flames. Somewhere out in the gathering darkness a coyote yowled and was answered by another coyote. The predators of the night were stirring from their lairs to prowl into the moonlight – to stalk and kill.

Morgan shivered. It seemed to the girl that dark forces were gathering. The Mortimers were coming – cousins to the Percys, dark mountain men – carrying guns and the smell of death with them.

Staring into the flames Morgan saw a form take shape in the flames. She gazed mesmerized while her eyes played tricks on her in the gloom and flickering firelight.

The shape and face of the tall youngster who had plunged so violently into her life moved and danced in the dying flames. He was looking directly at her, then he seemed to raise his hand and beckon to her.

Morgan was unable to move. She could not blink for fear of breaking the spell. He beckoned again to her then seemed to melt and change.

The crimson coals swirled and coalesced into the red beard of her brother. He was grinning out at her with that lopsided grin that so endeared him to her. His white teeth gleamed as coals shifted in the fire. As she watched, the red beard melted and the white of the teeth diffused out across the face. For a few terrifying moments a skull leered out at her obscenely then the coals fell in and a shower of sparks spiralled up towards the stars.

Morgan blinked and the spell was broken. She was back in the camp again. Beside her Harrison was quietly intent on building a smoke. He reached across and snatched a small partially burnt stick that had escaped from the fire and applied the glowing ember to the end of his cigarette. The images in the fire filled Morgan with dread premonition.

'Harrison, let's round up the herd and move on some-where else. They'll be well rested and fed now after time on this grass. We'll find somewhere better. Somewhere no one will want to fight over. I don't like it here. I have a bad feelin' about it.'

Harrison took a long draw at his cigarette before answering his sister.

'Morgan, you're fergittin' one thing. That rancher roped me an' dragged me. No one does that to a Percy – no one. That Grant fella has ta pay.'

'We're gonna reap nothin' here only ill-feeling and feudin',' Morgan said. 'We'll kill some of theirs and they'll kill some of ours. The townsfolk hate us. This rancher wants to drive us off his land that's rightfully his. Every hand in the region'll be against us. We moved home to start afresh. This ain't the way to do it. Killin' a man for his land ain't right.'

'You don't understand, Morgan. You're a woman. Men have things like honour an' pride and a name to uphold. If'n we run away from this fight then we'll never be able to hold up our heads again. Everywhere we go we'll be tagged with the yella brand. Folk will think they can do what they want agin us. They'll point at us and say – them there's the Percys – let's kick ass.'

'Honour an' pride,' Morgan said, in a weary voice, 'what good did honour an' pride do Pa when he rode off with the Mortimers to fight agin the Union? The best of our young men lie in graves across this great free land. Where's their honour an' pride? Years of fightin' broke us. Pa had to turn to rustlin' to build up his herd again.'

'Yeah, well, Pa only took back what was stole from him. He fought the war for a cause what he believed was right and proper. An' when the Yankees won they come an' plundered our land They turned us into rustlers. Pa could'a run away then but he didn't. He fought back the only way he could. He took back what was rightfully his.'

Morgan sighed. 'This land is so beautiful. I just drove up here through country so high, wide an' handsome it sometimes took my breath away. Yet we fight over every field. Every ditch an' waterway is filled with blood and hate. I just want to live in peace. See my children grow up without worryin' that someday they'll go off with their guns an' not come back. Is that an impossible dream?'

There was a long silence before Harrison spoke again.

'Sis, I don't know what it is you're sayin'. It seems to me I bin runnin' an' hidin' all my life. Well, I ain't runnin' from these sonsabitches.'

He stood and stretched mightily his jaws stretching wide in a prodigious yawn.

'Gawd, I need some shuteye. All this jawin' has me plumb wore out.'

He turned and trudged away leaving Morgan hunched before the dying fire. The reddish glow from the embers painted her face with an artificial radiance. The dull luminescence was reflected in her eyes and lit them up like rubies. They were the eyes of an ancient Indian goddess gazing back in time while at the same time glimpsing bits of the future.

9

The men were spread out among the pinewoods. All were heavily armed and carried Spencer repeating rifles as well as holstered Navy Colts and sheathed Bowie knives. There was no conversation nor did any of them light up a smoke. They were experts at hiding and skulking. So all sound was banned, as was odour of tobacco fumes.

To appease the craving a couple chewed wads of tobacco. Occasional venting of tobacco juice was the only noise from the hidden men. The sound of spitting easily lost across the distance to the trail they were keeping under surveillance.

The watchers wore long leather coats that reached well below the knees. Underneath these could be seen crossed bandoleers filled with shells. The oldest was a man in his fifties – with dark eyes set deep in his sockets. His high cheekbones and hollow cheeks gave him the aspect of a bird of prey. He jaws worked continuously and he spat with unvarying regularity.

A youngster sat several feet from him, his back against a tree bole. He constantly fiddled with the mechanism of his rifle as if he were anxious to be let loose on a shoot-ing spree. His beard was pale gold and matched his eyes that were pale and cold.

To either side of the pair were placed two large-boned men. Like the smaller man they were in their early twen-ties but there the similarities ended. One had thick coarse lips, bulbous nose and small piggy eyes. The other had regular well-defined features with a heavy, dark moustache growing on his upper lip.

The long, brown coats acted as excellent camouflage amongst the tangle of undergrowth and fallen branches. It was evident from the indolent ease of the men they were hunters – used to waiting patiently for the quarry to come within range of their guns. They were well spaced out amongst the trees. From this vantage point they could look down into the little valley that cut through the wooded slopes that seesawed across this range of hills. The men waited patient and confident.

Birds disturbed earlier by the arrival of the quartet cautiously began to reclaim their territory. A squirrel crept partway down his tree and alertly regarded the newcomers. Movement to his left caught the attention of the coarse-faced man.

He watched a moccasin glide within inches of his boot but did no more than draw his long bladed Bowie. The snake passed unmolested on some pursuit of its own. Then all idle movement amongst the watchers ceased. A subtle tenseness was evident, as the eyes became watch-ful. From the hills opposite, a body of horsemen had emerged.

The riders were spaced out along the trail. They rode slowly as if watchful for danger amongst the surrounding trees. Partway into the valley the leading horseman halted and dismounted. He knelt on the ground for a few moments, studying something on the trail. At last he turned and spoke to the men following him. As he talked he gestured and swept his arms about and from time to time pointed up the trail. He mounted and once more the party moved further into the valley.

Where the watchers waited, the valley rim dipped down as if a giant hammer had crashed down and made a small plateau. Because of its lower aspect the trees grew denser on this level. It meant the waiting men were only yards above the trail but well hidden in the tangled foliage.

Rifles inched forward. Fingers curled around triggers. Heads lowered and eyes squinted down barrels and gauged the distances. Otherwise there was no discernible movement amongst the group of four.

The riders came on steadily. Sharp eyes scanned the valley looking for signs of ambush. Watchful for birds fluttering up as a sigh of disturbance. Seeking the glint of a gun barrel amongst the tree line. Anything to indicate their quarry had gone to ground. Sixteen men rode into the valley of death, their eyes and hearts filled with killing lust and vengeance. In their midst rode a seventeenth man.

His hands were tied behind his back and he was hatless. Blood seeped from a bullet wound in his shoulder. His black hair hung unkempt and dusty about his blunt, square face. The face was bloody and swollen, evidence of a recent beating.

The posse had formed to chase the Mortimers after the gang entered the sanctity of their town and robbed the bank. No one had ever dared to come to Roanville and violate the town. That was until the Mortimer Gang rode in and dynamited the safe and rode off with $50,000. They had left three dead townsmen and would have escaped unscathed but for a lucky shot that had brought down Owen Grendon, the man now riding into the valley along with the posse – a bullet wound in his shoulder and his hands trussed.

The angry townspeople would have lynched Grendon there and then but for the urgency of following the rest of the gang and recovering the stolen money. They had to content themselves with kicking and punching the hapless bandit. Then roping him to a horse they had set out in hot pursuit.

A mocking bird gave its sudden and distinctive call. Owen Grendon sitting slumped in his saddle with his eyes half-shut, immediately tensed. His eyes snapped open and then he drove his heels hard into the flanks of his mount. The startled mare jumped forward but the horses in front hemmed her in. Other horses became excited at the sudden movement. Without exception all the riders in the posse turned to see what the disturbance was about.

In the pine woods Artie Mortimer sent a long stream of tobacco juice into the fallen leaves and sighted down the barrel of his Spencer.

10

The Grant family had just finished supper. Allison Grant was helping Melissa clear away the dishes. Hal got up from the table and stretched luxuriously. His dad looked over at him.

'Hal, can I have a word?'

'Sure, Pa,' Hal looked expectantly at his father.

'In private, son. We'll go out on the veranda. Will you all excuse us?'

Hal followed his father out on to the veranda. Night was settling across the land. A carpet of stars was beginning to weave its brightness across the sombre sky. Light from the bunkhouse spilled from an uncovered window with a soft yellow glow. Someone was gently strumming a guitar and quietly singing a love song. Harry Grant eased his big frame into a chair while Hal squatted on the veranda step.

'It's a beautiful place this, Hal – prime land for cattle and the most prosperous ranch in the area. It belongs to me and one day it'll all be yours.'

Hal said nothing. He knew this was leading up to something. His dad was simply warming up to whatever it was he wanted to talk about.

'The Grants have always been hard-workin', law-'bidin' citizens.'

Harry Grant paused again and still Hal waited. He heard a rustling behind him and smelt the faint scent of tobacco as his father built a smoke.

'Sheriff Blunt came out to the Big G today. I wasn't here but he talked to your mother.'

Hal reached down into the dirt of the yard and lifted a handful of dusty gravel. He sifted through the grains and flicked small pieces out into the darkness.

'He really wanted to speak to me, but you know Ma. She plied him with blueberry pie. Always said as the way to soften up a man is feed him.'

Hal guessed what was coming but could do nothing but sit and skip gravel out into the yard.

'Said as how Sheriff Blunt had some fellas dead to rights over some hold up or other. They claimed they couldn't have done robbery as they was with you in the Mule's Head at the time of the hold-up. Said as you would vouch for them.'

Harry Grant dragged deep on the cigarette. The coal glowed bright in the gloom of the veranda. He looked at the silent figure of his son.

'The sheriff was mighty peeved he had to let those villains go, on account he didn't want to go agin your word. Said as the word of a Grant was like Bible-true. What made him double sore was 'cos the man who had been robbed made a positive identification. He fingered a fat man who is a known criminal. Yet you were able to give him an alibi.'

As yet there was no response from Hal. Harry stared at

the back of the youngster as he sat on the steps, wondering if it was remorse or stubbornness that kept his son silent.

'I . . . I guess I wasn't thinkin' right right, Pa. It . . . it all started out as a bit of fun. I found out about the intended robbery. Then I hijacked the fellas as did it an' returned the money to the sheriff. I didn't think no harm in it.' The voice sounded miserable and contrite. 'Mebbe it were a dumb thing to do.'

'Hal . . . Hal,' the big man sighed deeply. 'I worry 'bout you. The Grant family have a name for straight dealin'.' Harry Grant paused before continuing, reluctant to bring up memories of past scandals. 'I had a cousin once. He did some evil things. I'm worried you is takin' after him.'

'Was that Richard, Pa?'

Now it was the turn of the older man to remain silent.

'You never would talk about that. In fact no one'll talk about Richard Grant – Ma nor Uncle Luke. What happened, Pa? Why cain't you tell me about him?'

'Its hard, son. It were a real bad time. Mebbe some day you an' I can go into town and if'n you git me drunk enough then I might just tell you the story.'

'I hear talk in the Mule's Head about it – mostly hearsay. Talk is you wiped out a nest of gunslingers single-handed. Is that true?'

Harry was not to know that his son, inspired by the tales of his father's legendary exploits, spent hours practising his gun skills. At first he used an old revolver with a worn mechanism donated to him by a ranch hand. This ancient relic as often as not misfired, frustrating his endeavours to become both fast and accurate. The gift of the new Colt on his eighteenth birthday had impelled him into greater efforts and his skills had sharpened dramatically.

In the gloom, the cigarette end glowed brightly.

'No, son. Fact is I had some help.' The glow from the cigarette blossomed again as Harry tried to draw some comfort from the weed. 'I suppose you gotta hear sometime. Better to come from me than some drunken rumour.'

Hal observed the spent butt sail out into the yard where it bounced in a shower of sparks and lay like the eye of some serpent balefully watching the two men on the veranda.

He could hear the rustle of the tobacco pouch and paper as his father prepared another smoke. The flare of the sulphur head lit the night for a moment before dying away.

As he waited, Hal aimed his pickles of gravel at the red glow of the discarded cigarette end. He waited for his father to speak wondering if he would ever hear the true story of his father's past. Behind him he could sense his father shift uneasily in his chair and nervously clear his throat.

11

'I guess I was about your age when it happened. This ranch meant a lot to me. I worked hard for your grand-dad. Didn't take much notice of what went on in town. Had a cousin, Richard Grant – owned about everything hereabouts. No one could ever prove it either way but when a couple of uncles were murdered, suspicion lighted on Richard. He fell heir to their wealth and prop-erties. Didn't know it at the time but he hankered after the Big G.' Hal sat quiet as his father paused to suck on his cigarette. 'Hired himself a gunslinger to remove the legitimate owners.'

'Granddad and you?'

'Yep, I gunned him down, but not before he put a bullet in your granddad.' Harry Grant sighed deeply. Unpleasant memories were being stirred up and his voice sank lower as he continued. 'He were a clever man, Cousin Richard. Hired himself a crooked sheriff and a judge. I went to prison for killin' that hired gun. An' while I was safely tucked away in prison Richard took over the Big G. But a good friend wangled a pardon an'

67

I was released. Again Richard sent gunmen after me.' To Hal's surprise his father chuckled. 'Your ma took care of 'em for me. She had herself a little derringer and she sure shot the hell outa those killers.'

'Pa, you're joshin' me!'

'Ain't, son. You ask your Uncle Luke. Your ma weren't gonna let no gunmen kill her future husband.' And Harry Grant grinned in the dark. 'Anyways, after that, I figured everything said about Richard was true. I knew he wouldn't stop till I was dead. So, along with some good friends I rode to the Hot Spur to have a showdown with Richard and his hired guns. Fortunately, Richard didn't survive.'

When he finished, Harry Grant sat staring out into the night with his son Hal seated by him. The silence was long – each man lost in his own thoughts.

'Pa.' Hal was first to break the silence. 'Thanks for tellin' me all this. I guess I've been a damned fool. I see now it weren't smart to hang out at the Mule's Head.'

'Hal, you're a Grant. We're a respected name in the community. The word of a Grant has to be solid gold. You ain't some low-born person to hang about with thieves an' wastrels. People have to look up to you. You're my son an' heir. What am I to say to folk as say to me, your son Hal is a liar and a thief?'

'Damnit, Pa, I know what you're saying. I . . . I guess it all seemed a bit of fun at the time but when you lay it on the line like that it ain't so funny. Leastaways not that bit 'bout family honour an' all.'

'OK, son. I ain't gonna mention it no more. Now to another serious matter. You know what's happening up at Potter's Creek with those hellions settling in there?

68

Fellas name of Percy. You know I had a run-in with them. Told them they're on private property an' gave 'em a week to move on. I got this gut feelin' they ain't gonna take any notice of my ultimatum. We're gonna have real trouble with those hellions.' Harry Grant paused in his recital. 'You heard anythin' about them?'

'Not much, Pa. Met a girl in town ran foul of Bill Gristy. She claims she's family to those there cowboys.'

'Gristy? Is that who roughed you up?' Harry asked shrewdly.

'Weren't nothin'. He was kinda stranglin' me when Morgan stepped in an' laid him out with the handle of her bullwhip.'

'Morgan, huh. She rescue you? Sounds a bit like your ma, savin' me from my cousin's gunhands. Guess you got kinda friendly with this gal?'

'Yeah, she was surely somethin'.'

'She know who you were?'

'No, Pa. I couldn't tell her my old man had ordered her brother off'n Big G land.'

Hal sounded miserable and Harry's heart went out to his son. It made him think of his own travails when he first met and fell for Allison.

'Hal, we got big trouble ahead. When I went to see them fellas I was hopin' to offer them some help gittin' their herd back on the trail again. There was no talkin' to them. The young'un, I guess he's this Morgan's brother you talk about, went for me. I had no option but to put him down. His friends went for their guns. I was lucky to git out from their camp with a whole skin. When this Morgan finds out the fella she rescued is the son of a sonovabitch as ordered them off the Big G she's gonna

69

SON OF A GUN

wish she'd let Gristy finish the job.'

'Jeez, Pa, you think I don't know that? When I realized she was one of the Percys I couldn't let on who I was.'

The door opened and a woman stepped softly on to the boards of the veranda. She carried a kerosene lamp and the glow illuminated the two men.

'You two finished jawing?' Allison asked.

Harry Grant looked down at his son. In the lamplight he could see the dejected slump of his son's shoulders.

'Your son's in love. Her name's Morgan Percy.'

'Percy! Why that's the rabble holed up at Potter's Creek. Oh, Hal, where'd you meet her?'

'Run into her in town,' Harry answered for his son. 'Sure is a bum hand fallin' for the sister of a trouble-maker.'

Allison set the lamp on a table. She went across to her son and seated herself beside him and put her arm around his shoulders.

'You really like this girl, Hal?'

'Mum, she's . . . she's beautiful. No one like her around here. Guess she'll come to hate me when she knows who I am.'

'When I first met your pa I never thought he would ever fall for me. But in spite of everything we ended up together.'

Hal suddenly turned to his mother. 'Ma, did you fight off some gunmen who were tryin' to kill Pa?'

'Who told you that?'

'Pa did.'

It was Allison's turn to stare out into the starlight night. She took a moment or two before replying.

'It wasn't quite like that, but yes, I did shoot a very bad

man. If you truly love someone, you'll let nothing stand in the way.' She paused, then said softly, '*Alas, that love, so gentle in his view, should be so tyrannous and rough in proof.*'

12

Long into the night Hal lay and fretted. Sleep would not come as he tossed and turned, going over and over in his mind the conversation he'd had with his father and mother. He squirmed as he remembered his father's words about family honour and pride. His shenanigans in town had gone a long way to besmirching the family name.

At times he broke into a cold sweat as he remembered some of the stunts he and his shady companions from the Mule's Head had pulled. The hold-up at Preachers Wood had shown him what a disreputable crowd he mixed with and how low he himself had sunk.

Thinking about it now he realized how horribly wrong things could have gone. Armed robbery was a serious offence. Then to compound his crimes he had lied to Sheriff Blunt.

Even as he had vouched for his crooked companions he could see the contempt in the lawman's eyes. Only the fact he was Harry Grant's son had prevented the sheriff from throwing him out into the street or even slinging him into a cell.

The Mule's Head gang had welcomed him because he was the son of a wealthy rancher. He was a young man of means with money to spend. When the time came for him to inherit the Big G all his hangers-on would expect favours from him. He thought of the hard-working ranch hands he toiled with on the ranch. Somehow he could not see Falmouth and his cronies putting in the same effort as his father's faithful cowhands.

Most of the Mule's Head crowd spent their days plotting their next act of villainy. Thievery, trickery, cheating at cards, the odd foray out on to the range to steal a few head of livestock. It seemed no business was too shameful for the low-life clustered around the Mule's Head. And he, Hal Grant, had revelled in these villainous deeds and at times had even joined in.

As he lay sleepless, wrestling with all these things, Hal came to the conclusion he would have to make things right with his dad. As soon as he could decently slip away he would go to Potter's Creek and talk to the Percys. Maybe his father had been a bit too blunt when he visited them. He could try and reason with the newcomers. And there was also an added incentive: it would be an excuse to see Morgan.

Hal set his cowpony towards Potter's Creek. There was no hurry to his errand so he allowed his pony to canter at a steady pace while he pondered over what he could do and say to bring about some sort of peace. Eventually he saw the telltale smoke from the camp-fire and still without any plan he rode towards the creek.

As he drew near he could see a reception committee riding out to meet him. A couple of riders were spurring their mounts across the creek. He halted his pony and sat quietly holding up his hand, palm out, in the universal gesture of peace.

The horsemen pulled up and surrounded Hal. The men were armed with Winchesters held loosely across the pommels of their saddles. Their faces bore no friendliness towards the lone rider. It seemed to Hal these were men expecting trouble and quite prepared to use the guns they held so casually.

'Howdy, fellas. You sure look loaded for bear. I was only ridin' by for a visit.'

'What's your business, cowboy? You lookin' fer somethin' in particular?' The tone was unfriendly as were the hard eyes staring out at him from below floppy hat brims. The man who had spoken was a lean-faced man with a scar running down one side of his face. It made him look sinister and threatening.

'I was hopin' to see the boss of this here outfit.'

The riders were circling Hal. He sat still, momentarily wondering what he had got himself into. One of the cowboys leaned forward in his saddle and pointed at the brand on Hal's mount.

'Gawddamn it. The son of a bitch rides for the Big G.' The Winchesters snapped up so they covered Hal. He sat very still keeping his hands in sight. It had not occurred to him to wear his gunbelt. He was only intending a visit to the Percys, with the idea of patching up some sort of compromise between his dad and Morgan's family. Of course, a powerful incentive had been the possibility of renewing his acquaintance with the girl.

'I ain't heeled. I didn't ride over here lookin' for trouble. I just come on a social visit. You fellas appear mighty unfriendly.'

'Less of the lip, cowboy. Just ride over yonder. We'll see what the boss has to say 'bout Big G riders on visits. Don't sit right with us. Your boss acted mighty unfriendly on his last visit. So just you ride towards the camp.'

Hal said nothing. He kicked his mount forward and rode towards the creek with his armed escort.

As he grew closer, Hal could see a lot of work had been done. The foundations of a storehouse had been laid out along with various outbuildings. These constructions were made of sturdy hewn logs and the camp was a hive of industry.

Two men were operating a ripsaw while others were trimming logs and still others were laying them in place. Corrals had been erected for livestock and a sturdy oven had been built. The camp cook could be seen working with his pots. The invigorating smell of coffee and baking bread mingled with wood smoke and fresh sawdust.

Hal's heart sank as he surveyed all this activity. These *hombres* were not expending all this energy just to pull up stakes and move on.

He began to wonder if he had ridden out on a fool's errand. But the thought of the raven-haired young woman he met in Lourdes stiffened his resolve. If nothing else at least he would get to see her again and who knew what would come of that meeting? That was the real objective of his trip.

As he rode up to the encampment his eyes searched in vain for the ox-drawn wagon. Men halted work to watch the riders. Hal noticed the Winchesters placed handy to the labourers. An older man with a drooping, grey-speckled moustache detached himself from a group of workers and ambled over to the riders.

'Howdy, Al,' he greeted the scar-faced man. 'Whaddaya got here?'

'Dunno, Boss. Rides a Big G cowpony. I reckon he's a scout sent to spy out the camp. Sons of bitches could be set on hittin' us sometime soon.'

It struck Hal then that this was not just an ordinary encampment. These men were planning for a siege. The evidence was there before him: the rifles to hand, the sturdy log buildings, the scouts riding out to scrutinize strangers. This place was being run like a military compound.

'You ride for the Big G?' the veteran said to Hal. 'We had a visit from your boss a few days ago. He roughed up my son, Harrison and then threw down on us. Lucky fer us he wasn't a very good shot.'

'Doesn't sound like Harry Grant to me. He's a peace-lovin' kinda man. You musta done somethin' to rile him.'

'You sayin' I'm a liar, boy?'

'Look, Mr Percy, I ain't come here lookin' for trouble. I was hoping we could talk a mite and patch things up 'tween us.'

Tom Percy spat between the forelegs of Hal's pony. As he was about to reply a commotion from the creek distracted him. Three riders were spurring across the river, churning up the water in waves around the horses' legs. It seemed the whole camp paused to watch the newcomers.

The horses clambered up the shallow river-bank and

cantered towards Hal's little group. He noticed the leading rider had a close-cropped red beard and realized this must be Harrison Percy, Morgan's brother.

13

'Take the horses down first. Don't worry about killin'
'em. Just bring 'em down on the floor. Ed an' me'll take
the front. You two hit the rear end. Make every shot
count. After that it'll be a turkey shoot.' Artie Mortimer
shifted the wad of tobacco in his mouth. 'An' I don't
need to tell you, any of 'em bastards as much as looks like
he might take a pot shot at Owen, I won't be mad if'n you
use a whole belt of bullets to keep him safe.'

The orders were given like a captain in the army
instructing his troops how to behave in a forthcoming
battle. Indeed Artie Mortimer had learned his killing
trade during the War Between the States. Only he had
not fought in regular units. He had chosen to fight
under Quantrill and his guerrillas.

Now the leader of his little band squeezed trigger and
the shot cracked out echoing across the valley as he sent
the first bullet into the agitated riders below.

The Sheriff of Roanville led the posse. Determined to
show the citizens of the town he was an efficient lawman,
he had pursued the fleeing bank robbers with the tenac-
ity of a bloodhound on a trail.

He had twisted around in his saddle in order to see what was causing the commotion behind him when the prisoner's horse rammed into its fellows. In this position he faced the hidden shooters square on. Even though Artie Mortimer had instructed his sons to aim for the horses he could not resist the broad target the sheriff presented. The bullet entered the law-officer's chest, punctured a lung and flung him back out of the saddle. Almost as he fired Mortimer was traversing the sights to the next rider in the procession.

Artie Mortimer had trained his sons well. They aimed and fired – aimed and fired, in a precise and orderly manner. The result was a deadly hail of lead raking the riders on the trail below.

Horses screamed and plunged as bullets hammered home into equine heads, necks and flanks. Several riders and horses went down under the first salvo. Men trying to extract guns from saddle scabbards had difficulty as their distraught mounts leapt and plunged in the valley bottom. Wounded horses screamed as the bullets hammered home. Some were on the ground squealing in agony and trapping their riders or injuring others as they thrashed around in pain-induced panic.

In the midst of this carnage, Owen Grendon turned his mount and, using his knees and heels, urged it towards the opposite slope. The remaining members of the posse were too occupied with their own perilous plight to take much notice of the captive.

Grendon's horse, spooked by the dreadful screaming and bloodletting around it, took off up the incline in a panic-maddened lunge. It did not get far before it was labouring, for the grade was quite steep. Grendon did not mind. He was content to await developments as the gun battle raged behind him.

Fallen horses and men littered the trail along which they had just a few minutes ago trotted so confidently. On the opposite slope he could see a haze of bluish smoke drifting up from a group of pine trees.

The ambush site had been well chosen and with no prior warning the posse members had been unable to take evasive action. They were being cut to pieces as the four marksmen kept up a vicious barrage of rifle fire.

A few men had managed to unlimber guns and take shelter behind fallen horses. They fired sporadically towards the trees. Aiming uphill and not being able to see what they were firing at, their shooting was desultory and uncoordinated. Anyone trying to aim and fire up at the killers immediately became the target for a hail of bullets. If not immediately hit they ducked low and could only poke weapons in the general direction of the attackers and fire without aiming.

The hail of fire was relentless. Downed horses and men were hit again and again as bullets smashed into dead and dying flesh. Then suddenly from out of that hell of dying and dead horses and men, an arm could be seen waving a rifle stock in the air and yelling something that was lost in the crescendo of gunfire.

'Hold your fire,' Artie Mortimer called out. He had to yell again before his brood ceased. The gunfire died and in the relative silence the men in the pinewoods could feel their ears buzzing. Below them, horses still squealed in pain and terror and injured men were crying out for help.

'Gawddamn it, Pa, I'm only just gittin warmed up.'

Artie spat a long stream of juice towards the besieged men. 'They're tryin' to tell us somethin'. Mebbe they've had enough. Go on, Bull. Ask 'em what they wants.'

The coarse-featured youngster laid down his weapon and formed his hands into a funnel. 'What's up, lawmen? You had enough yet?' he bellowed.

'We give up. There's a lot of wounded men an' horses down here. For mercy's sake, give us a chance. We cain't fight anymore.'

'Tell them to throw away their weapons an' stand up with hands in the air.'

There was some movement amongst the dead and dying and eventually five men rose from the horror of the carnage around them. They stood helplessly, listening to wounded friends and neighbours calling for help.

None of the attackers had shown himself yet.

The five beaten men stood looking up at the pinewoods from which the barrage of lead had come. Out of the sixteen men who had ridden out on a trail of vengeance these few were the only ones relatively unscathed.

'OK, boys. Bull an' Dick, you go down there and reconnoitre the situation. Keep well outa the line of fire. Ed an' me'll cover you. Any funny business, you just drop to the floor and we all blast away.'

The youngsters rose from their hiding place and walking well wide of the original firing positions began a slow cautious descent of the slope. The stench of spilled blood and gunsmoke rose up to meet them as they moved downhill. Wounded men were still calling for help and injured animals thrashed and squealed in agony.

The men in the midst of the slaughter watched with dull eyes as their attackers approached. They were apprehensive of these men after the shockingly brutal way their party had been cut down.

At the bottom of the slope, the youngsters surveyed the scene of devastation. They sensed there was no more fight left in the survivors.

'OK, Pa. Looks like we won the battle.'

Artie Mortimer along with Ed, came down the slope to join his other two sons. Owen Grendon nudged his mount and it nervously made its way back down to the trail.

'Howdy, Artie, wondered when you would show up.'

The hawk-faced man looked up at the mounted man.

'That blood on your shirt, Owen? You hurt bad?'

'It'll heal. You got your Bowie handy? I'm a mite tired of being tied to this here horse.'

'Your face is all mashed up, Owen,' Bull observed, as he obligingly moved over and cut the ropes around Grendon's wrists and ankles. Indeed, Owen's face was a mass of cuts and bruises and congealed blood.

As the freed man massaged his wrists he glared malignantly at the surviving members of the posse.

'These bastards worked me over some. Were goin' to hang me but decided to chase after you instead. They had it in mind to hang us all together.'

Shots rang out as Ed and Dick Mortimer walked through the blood-soaked battleground. Every now and then they would stop by a wounded horse and place the Spencer against it temple and pull the trigger. When they finished the gruesome task the only sound was the cries of the wounded men.

'Cain't we take care of the wounded?' a burly man with blood on his face asked.

By now Grendon had dismounted. He took the Bowie from Bull and tested the edge.

'I reckon you were the son of a bitch kicked me in the crotch,' he said, as he walked across to the speaker. 'Had my hands tied an' you took advantage of a helpless man.'

'Weren't me, mister. Musta been some of these other boys. You gonna let us look after these poor wounded men now?'

'These poor wounded men were gonna hang us all when you caught up with us. What sorta justice you call that? Weren't even gonna have a trial?' He turned to his rescuers who stood in a circle watching with grins on their faces. 'They even brung along ropes. Gonna lynch us they was. Without even the benefit of a preacher to shrive our misbegotten souls. We'da gone straight to hell on the end of them hangin' ropes.'

'Mister, we weren't gonna do no such thing. We was gonna bring you back to face trial in Roanville.'

'Help . . . please help me . . .' a voice called faintly.

Bull turned round and spotted some movement among the bodies. 'Gawddamn fella here's gotta star on his vest.'

The outlaws gathered round and stared curiously at the wounded sheriff. He was lying on his back. Crimson stained the front of his shirt and blood bubbled from nose and mouth. His lips opened and more crimson frothed as he tried to speak again. 'Help . . . me . . .'

'You hurt, Sheriff?' Bull bent over the body as he spoke. He used the toe of his boot to open the man's vest wide. A wet stain in the lawman's chest oozed blood every time he breathed.

The man's pain-glazed eyes stared up at the youngster. 'Help . . .' he whispered again.

'My, my, that does look bad. You need a doctor.' Bull looked across at the men still standing with hands raised. 'Any of you fellas a sawbones?' he asked.

All shook their heads.

'Sorry, Sheriff, no sawbones. I guess I'll just have to treat you myself.' He placed the Spencer against the wounded man's forehead and pulled the trigger. As the bullet smashed through the bone into the brain, the sheriff's body jerked once and was still. The top of the head disappeared in a welter of blood and splintered bone.

'Oh my God!' someone gasped.

Bull reached down and plucked the star from the dead-man's vest. Grinning at his companions, he pinned the badge of office on to his coat. He looked across to the survivors. 'Any of you fellas got objection to me takin' on the sheriff's job?' He aimed the Spencer at the little group. Some of the men cringed back trying to shrink their bodies into smaller targets as the rifle traversed them. 'Seems to me like nobody's objectin'.'

'Seems to me, Sheriff, these fellas here are outside the law. They was fixin' to hang these men,' Owen Grendon swept his hand around at the rest of the Mortimer family, 'without a proper trial. Now that seems dang right criminal in my eyes. How do you fellas feel about it?'

Artie Mortimer spat a long stream of tobacco juice towards the frightened captives. He turned and winked at Dick and Ed Mortimer. 'Members of the jury, these fellas are accused of unlawfully takin' the law into their own hands with the unlawful intention of hangin' a person or persons unknown without a proper trial. Members of the jury, what's your verdict?'

'Guilty!' the brothers called out gleefully.

'Owen, seeing as you're a material witness you'll have to pass sentence. Us Mortimers might just be a mite prejudiced agin' these here criminal types.'

'Wa-al,' Grendon said thoughtfully, as he repeatedly tossed the Bowie knife in the air, 'I was shot and then beat up by these upright citizens. They wanted to hang me. Now I would say, hangin's too good for them.' He sauntered over to a downed horse and reached for the saddle. 'Lookee here, they even brung along their own ropes. Now that's what I call real intent.'

One of the captured men dropped to his knees. 'Look, fellas, you've had your fun. Let us attend to the wounded. We ain't gonna to bother you no more.'

Owen Grendon turned cold, merciless eyes on the speaker. 'Fun! The fun ain't started yet! We're gonna have a party. An' you're invited. In fact you're all invited. We're gonna have us a hog-stickin' party.'

14

'Git that rope up on that branch.'

The rider angled his mount forward until he was beneath the cottonwood. With practised ease he shook out the coils of the rope. The end curled up and over the stout branch on the first throw. There was a cheer from the onlookers. They were gathered around the edge of the trees, their work all but forgotten at the prospect of some fun.

Hal peered through swollen eyes at the cowboy as the man turned and grinned back at his companions. Blood ran from Hal's nose and stained his shirt. A gash on his cheek also dripped blood. His lips were cut and bruised – his eyes swollen and almost closed. But for the men on each side holding him upright he might have collapsed.

His attempts at peacemaking had been doomed from the moment Morgan's brother found out who he was.

'No son of a bitch comes in here an' pushes us around.' Percy had snarled just before he punched Hal in the face. Hal had only managed one punch in retaliation before Percy's men pinioned his arms.

'Hold him up,' the red-bearded man had instructed

his men. Systematically he then proceeded to hammer Hal into a bloody pulp.

'Your bastard dad won't recognize you when I've finished with you,' he had grunted as he punched with all his force into Hal's stomach.

Hal gasped and, but for his minders holding him, would have gone down.

'You yella snake,' Hal panted, as he sucked in his breath. 'You cain't face me as a man, one to one—'

A hard fist smashed into his eye and drove his head back.

'You're just a puppy dog,' his tormentor taunted. 'I don't need to prove myself agin a whelp like you.'

Regaining his breath Hal judged when the next blow was due and using the support of the two men holding on to him he brought up his boot. It was perfectly timed. His toe drove hard up into Percy's groin. Hal had put all his force into the kick. Percy folded and as his head came over Hal's other foot smashed into his face. The stricken man went down like he was pole-axed.

'Son of a bitch,' one of the men holding Hal swore, as he saw his boss go down. Hurriedly they hauled their captive out of range as Hal attempted to bring his heel down on the fallen man's head. As it was, his spur dug a bloody line across the man's skull.

Percy lay on the ground retching. Blood poured from the gash in his scalp.

'Jesus, he'll kill you for sure,' the man informed Hal.

Tom Percy came across and helped his son to sit up. The younger man's face was drained of colour. His red beard was stark against the bloodless face. He groaned and folded his hands across his groin. Agony was etched in every line of his youthful face. His breath was ragged as he tried to contain the pain.

'Son of a bitch . . .' he at last managed to gasp. 'You're gonna pay for that, Grant. You're gonna pay . . .'

Tom was helping him to his feet. Hal watched with some satisfaction as Harrison bent over double, finding it difficult to stand upright. It was some minutes before the injured man was able to gather enough strength to limp over to Hal. Tears streaked his face and blood leaked from his mashed mouth where Hal's boot had connected.

Hal tensed his body in readiness for the punches that he expected. But the bearded man stood glaring balefully at him. He made no attempt to continue the punishment he had started. For a few moments the hate-filled eyes stared at Hal.

'Tie his hands.'

Hal was trussed as directed and helplessly awaited the thrashing he expected from the injured Harrison Percy.

'Fetch a rope.'

It was only when the whole party moved to the trees and the exercise with the rope that Hal began to suspect what the bearded youngster was up to.

'Son of a bitch,' he whispered through swollen lips. But he suspected the men wanted to frighten him. That they had any intention of carrying out a hanging was unthinkable.

'Bring his horse.'

As he oversaw the preparations Harrison leant heavily on his father. His discomfort was evident as, painfully, he limped to the grove of trees. Hal ardently wished his hands were free and he and Harrison Percy were alone.

'I's gonna kill thass yella snake,' he muttered thickly. His captors could not make out the words, as Hal mumbled through cut and bruised lips.

'Git him up there.'

Willing hands pushed Hal to his horse and lifted him into the saddle. Harrison came across and gripped Hal's leg. Malevolent eyes stared up at him.

'Git that rope round his neck.'

The mounted cowboy who had slung the rope over the branch brought his horse alongside Hal and, grinning, arranged the noose and pulled it tight. With his hands trussed and his leg held by Percy there was nothing Hal could do to prevent this happening. He stared defiantly down at Percy.

'Soffabisch.' His words were indistinct as he tried to get his mouth to work. 'I's cut your 'art ous. It'll 'urt worss'n yore ball-sss.'

'Bastard! You won't be doin' nothin' no more. I'm gonna hang you, an' then tie your dead body on your horse an' send you back to your bastard father. Then I'm gonna hang him. An' as he gasps out his last rotten breaths I'll give your mother an' sisters to my men. The last thing your old man'll see is his womenfolk having a good time with my boys. He'll fry in Hell with that thought in his mind.'

There was a cheer from the gathered cowhands. And it was then Hal began to realize this may not be a jest construed to frighten him. He looked into the eyes of his opponent and what he saw confirmed his worst suspicions.

'Yis is murder. The lawss'll come affer yous. If yous carry out thish hangin' youss'll end up hangin' yourselfs.'

For answer Harrison Percy took out his Colt revolver. Grinning up at his victim malevolently he cocked the gun.

'Just watch me, you son of a bitch. You won't have long to wait for the rest of your family to join you in Hell.'

Pointing the muzzle of the gun into the air he pulled the trigger. Hal's mount lurched forward. He tried to hold on to the saddle with his thighs but the pony's forward movement was unstoppable. To cheers from the onlookers Hal swung free of the pony.

The swinging weight of his unsupported body tightened the noose about his neck. He gasped and tried to gulp some air but his windpipe was constricting. Then he was swaying back and forth as the rope cut off his air supply. Spiralling freely on the end of the rope, slowly he began to strangle.

For the second time in a few days Hal Grant was being choked to death. His eyes bulged and his face, already swollen from his beating, became suffused with blood. A bright light was shining into his eyes. For moments, he was sensible of a kaleidoscope of branches, leaves and snatches of blue sky – then darkness – blessed darkness.

The men gathered to witness the hanging become subdued as they watched the results of their exertions. There were no more ribald jests. They stared restless and troubled as the body of Hal Grant swayed gently on the end of the rope. Tom Percy stepped forward.

'OK, boys, I'm sure he's learnt his lesson. Cut him down.'

As he spoke urine dribbled from the heel of the hanging youth's boots.

Suddenly Harrison Percy thrust his face hard into that

of the old man's.

'Gawddamn it, Pa, that's Grant's son hangin' there. Cain't you see what this'll do to him? Strike hard an' fast at the enemy. That's what Uncle Mortimer allus told us. Grant'll come at us like a mad bull. That's when we'll git him.'

'Jeez, Harrison, he's only a kid . . .'

The rumble of wheels interrupted any further exchange. The hanging party turned and watched the arrival of the wagon drawn by four oxen.

15

With Owen Grendon supervising, the Mortimer boys had secured the remaining members of the posse to separate pine trees.

'This is fun, ain't it fellas?' Owen Grendon grinned at the prisoners.

No amount of pleading by the survivors had moved the Mortimers. Owen Grendon took particular relish in taunting the posse members as they pleaded for mercy.

'If'n I spare you, will you in return give me a night of passion with your wife and daughters?'

'Yes, gawddamn it. But my daughter's only twelve. My wife's a fine big woman.'

'Twelve's a mite old for me, but I'll try her out for you.'

The Mortimer boys roared with delight. 'What 'bout us, Owen? We'll have the girl. You can have the old lady.'

'I only got sons,' another man whined. 'Ain't got no wife.'

'Well, long as they're young an' tender we don't mind. Was so desperate once when I was on the run, had to make do with a sheep.'

This was too much. The Mortimers roared with laughter and slapped their thighs.

'Gawddamn, Owen, If'n you don't take the biscuit,' Artie Mortimer called out.

'Jeez, Owen,' Bull stared at Grendon with his protruding eyes, 'Did you really? I mean, what were that like?'

His brothers were hysterical now. Ed was bent over double as he hooted with laughter. Dick had to hold on to the pommel of one of the few horses that had survived the shootout.

Owen Grendon winked across at Bull. 'We-ll, mebbe when we're alone sometime I'll tell ya.'

'Will ya, Owen?'

Even dour Artie Mortimer, seated on a fallen tree trunk, had his hand curled about his mouth as he tried to hide his mirth. Artie usually tried to shield his slow-witted son from brotherly ribbing, but the mirth was infectious and he could do nothing to help Bull as Owen reeled him in like an over-eager fish.

'Mind you, ya gotta select your sheep. Sheep is like dogs or women – too young an' they's too frisky – too old an' they's ornery.'

The explosion of laughter distracted Bull from his eager search for titillation. He looked at his two brothers, by now helpless with mirth. Even Artie had abandoned all attempts to conceal his laughter.

'Gawddamn, what's so funny, assholes?' Bull glared at his brothers. He had forever been the butt of many a joke and suspected now that somehow his two brighter brothers were taking advantage of him. But for the life of him he could not figure what the joke was.

'Enough, enough,' Artie called out, struggling to keep his voice from cracking as he tried to restrain the laughter from bubbling out of control again. 'We cain't spend all day discussin' the love life of sheep.'

That remark only made things worse. Nothing could stop the tide of mirth from Ed and Dick. Both were helpless now and tears rolled down their cheeks. Artie abandoned all attempts to control them.

'Git on with it, Owen, we ain't got all day.'

Even as they went about their ghoulish work every time either of the brothers caught sight of Bull they broke into giggles. The screams of the victims added a bizarre background to the sounds of merriment.

Only one man defied the gang's attempt to humiliate him. He was a tall lanky man with a lean, tanned face. Blood stained the side of his head where a bullet had grazed his skull. When Owen Grendon stood before him with his Bowie knife at the ready he glared scornfully back at the outlaw.

'Gawddamn mudsills, one day the law'll catch up with you. You'll swing on the end of a rope.'

'You won't be around to testify even if that happens.' Owen grinned wickedly as he drove the big blade into the man's midriff. He heaved upwards. The man's mouth opened but no sound emerged. He slumped forward as the blade was pulled clear. Only the rope binding him to the tree held him upright. Blood pumped from the fearsome wound that was opened in his stomach. The sharp steel had sliced from his bellybutton to his breastbone. Owen stepped back and admired his handiwork.

'Hope you ain't too cut up about all this. But I'll say this much – you got guts.'

Owen wiped his blade on the man's jacket. He turned to observe his companions as they executed their victims.

The screams of the surviving posse members told of worse things being done to them. Owen grinned in approval.

'That's the way, boys. Your old pa sure taught you right. My one regret is my career nor my temperament did not give me marriage nor children. I would have been proud to have whelped pups like you lot. We could have teamed up together and with such a force we would have driven the damn Yankee army all the way back to Washington.'

The wretched victims hung from the ropes binding them to the tree-trunks. None of the men were to die as quickly and as easily as had Owen's victim. The screams echoed through the trees startling birds and small mammals and sent them fleeing from the human animals inflicting such horror on their fellow human beings.

Bull was trying to scalp his victim. After making the incision around the moaning man's head he tugged hard at a handful of hair. There was a tearing sound and Bull staggered back. He never regained his balance and sat down. 'Gawddamn!' In his hand was a bloodied scalp.

When Bull sat down his brothers quit their own knife work. Once more their laughter echoed among the pine trees mixing bizarrely with the shrieks of their victims.

It was another half-hour before the last screams died away.

Leaving the valley of death behind them, the outlaws rode north-east. They were well satisfied with the results of their endeavours. Only Grendon was morose as he nursed his wounded shoulder. Artie Mortimer had cleaned and dressed the wound before they set out declaring himself satisfied it was not too serious.

They camped that night in an abandoned shack. No fire was lit and they dined on jerky and cold beans. Next day's dawn was hardly breaking when they set out again. Their destination was Jarrod's Cross – a handful of buildings that had grown up around a crossroads.

16

The morning after her arrival in the encampment Morgan rose early before anyone was up and about. She made her way along the creek till she was out of sight of the camp and, stripping off, washed herself all over while standing knee deep in the creek.

The water was cold and she shivered as she performed her toilet. When she arrived back at the camp the cook was up and had stirred some life into the fire. Gratefully she sat before the warmth and waited for the hot coffee to be served. Over breakfast of sowbelly and bread she sat with her family.

'Pa, what can I do to make myself useful?' she asked, as she chewed at the fried bread.

'We're runnin' short of supplies. However, I don't want to go into Lourdes. Let that place simmer down a mite before we venture in there. When we do go we'll go in a bunch. But we're busy here. Cain't spare an escort. There's a small settlement 'ween here an' Toska. Should be able to git most things there.'

Morgan asked for help to unload the wagon. The canvas cover was folded and stored. With the wagon now converted Morgan harnessed up her oxen.

'See you at supper,' she yelled to the menfolk. The bullwhip snapped over the backs of the sturdy beasts. The wagon lumbered into motion and Morgan set out on her trip to bring back supplies for the camp.

It had been a successful trip. The settlement was no more than a cluster of buildings. A store, two taverns, a blacksmith who doubled as carpenter and undertaker catered for a farming community edged out by the big ranchers in the region. Fresh produce was readily available along with dried goods and, most importantly, from the men's viewpoint back at the encampment, a case of corn whiskey.

Morgan indulged herself by purchasing a new cotton shirt and a spare pair of jeans. Unlike most western women she preferred to wear male apparel. It made sense to drive a team of oxen in practical work jeans rather than hinder movement by the wearing of long skirts and petticoats.

Arriving back from her errand she was hot, tired, dusty and irritable. She saw the men gathered around the small group of cottonwoods and angled her team over in their direction. At first she did not notice the object of their attentions. She popped her bullwhip and yodelled a greeting. The men stirred apart slightly but did not return her greeting. Then she saw the figure hanging from the tree.

'Aw, God! Jesus Gawd, what the hell's goin' on?'

A feeling of dread stabbed into the pit of her stomach. For a moment the wagon carried on towards the terrible scene unattended. She had forgotten the bullwhip and the reins gripped in knuckle-white hands. The vacuous faces of the men stared back at her as the oxen lumbered forward.

'Jesus Christ!' The expletive came out as a yell. Abruptly she stood upright in the wagon and the bull-whip snaked out.

'Yip, yip, yip!' she screamed as she spurred on the team. The snapping whip and Morgan's yells startled the oxen out of their slow amble. They bellowed and surged forward. She ignored the men scattering from the path of the heavy beasts. With instinctive skill she brought the wagon to a halt beneath the hanging man.

Morgan did not know the identity of the man hanging on the end of the rope. She was acting purely on impulse now. Standing on the wagon's seat she was almost level with the man's chest. The Bowie knife she always carried was in her hand. She was not conscious of retrieving the knife.

It took only a quick slash with the keen blade and the man tumbled into her arms. She tried to let him down gently but fell back into the body of the wagon with the dead weight on top of her. The wind was punched out of her. With a tremendous push she heaved the body from her. Next instant she was kneeling by the man and sawing at the rope around his neck. As she worked she sobbed aloud, racked with shock and disbelief at what had happened.

She had to be careful not to cut the man's neck. The rope had embedded itself in the flesh. Blood seeped from the bruised, skinned neck. Just as the rope parted and fell away Harrison's face appeared over the side of the wagon.

'Sis, what the hellya doin'?'

'Git away from here,' she hissed. The anger in her voice was unmistakable.

Harrison blinked. 'For Gawd's sake, Morgan, it's Grant's son – Grant – the rancher what wants to throw us of'n here!'

'I don't give a damn who he is!' Her voice had risen.

He flinched before her anger but went on relentlessly.

'Leave him be. We're sendin' his dead body back to his old man. It'll teach him not to mess with us Percys.'

'Gawddamn it, Harrison, since when did we become a lynch mob? It'll make us murderers.'

Her eyes flicked back to the body on the floor of her wagon. It was only then she took note of the man she had cut down. Despite the mottled skin and the blood and mucus on his face she recognized the boy she had met only recently.

'Jesus H. Christ, Harrison. Have you gone mad?' she whispered.

Harrison reached a hand out to grip his sister's arm. Without thinking she punched him full in the face. He disappeared from sight. She turned her attention back to the boy.

'Please don't be dead,' she pleaded.

On instinct she placed her mouth on the boy's lips and blew hard. Then she slammed her palms down on his chest. Again she repeated the treatment. She was weeping as she worked. There was shouting from outside the wagon but she ignored this. She thought she could hear her father's raised voice. Something slammed against the side of the wagon making it rock slightly. But she was oblivious to everything else as she worked on the unconscious boy. Then his body twitched and a long

SON OF A GUN

shuddering sigh escaped from his broken lips.

'Oh God, please let him live,' Morgan prayed. She held his face gently in her hands. The breath was ragged but it was working of its own accord. Then he began to shake as if with ague.

On the back of the seat was an old blanket. Morgan grabbed this and quickly wrapped it round the quivering youth. She leapt into the front and scooped up the reins.

'Yip, yip, yip!' she yelled. The bullwhip snapped out and the wagon began to circle away from the trees. 'Faster, faster,' she screamed and the bullwhip snapped and popped lending urgency to her commands.

'Morgan, Morgan,' someone yelled out. 'What the hellya doin?'

'Faster, faster, you sons of bitches.'

'Morgan, for Chris'sake, stop this gawddamn wagon!' Harrison Percy was running alongside the lumbering wagon. 'Morgan stop, or I'll shoot.'

Morgan glanced sideways at her brother. He was hatless and running with the wagon. She noticed the gun in his hand seconds before he fired. The barrel of the revolver was pointed in the air. In spite of this she ducked in fright and almost lost her grip on the reins. It was with pure reflex action the coils of the bullwhip snaked out. The lead-weighted tip snapped across her brother's gun hand. Abruptly he dropped out of sight.

Then the vehicle gathered speed as the oxen, frightened by the gunshot, took off at a fear-maddened run.

'On, on, you great lumps of shit,' she yelled at the beasts. Then she was hanging on to the reins and sobbing as the wagon drew further and further from her family. She was frightened to look back. Frightened of what she had just witnessed and frightened for the boy wrapped in the old blanket in the back of her wagon.

'Faster, faster,' she whispered. She had no more energy to call out aloud. But the great beasts were running of their own accord now, throwing up sods of dirt as they pounded across the grassland. The wind of their passage gusted in her face and blew her tears back into her dark hair.

'Dear God, don't let him die,' she sobbed. 'I'm sorry I got angry. And I'm sorry I swore. Just please, please, don't let him die.'

17

Jarrod's Cross was a safe haven for men on the run. Here they could obtain food, drink and supplies. Horses could be fed and watered or exchanged for better mounts.

It was also a meeting place and post office for men outside the law. It was a place to leave messages for friends and relatives. They could catch up on news and learn where the quick money was to be had.

There was an added luxury for men used to spending days in the saddle and sleeping rough. At night they would sleep in a proper bed and with a roof over their heads.

Another day's hard riding brought the Mortimers within sight of the settlement. Wearily they rode in. Now they could relax and spend some of the money they had stolen from Roanville.

They arranged stabling and feed for their mounts. The unharmed horses from the doomed posse had been brought along. These would be sold or exchanged for better mounts. Their horses seen to, the gang headed for the Devil's Kitchen.

*

Douglas Earl was a huge man. His mother had been a black prostitute working in the brothels of California. His father had been an Irishman who had sailed the seven seas until news of the gold tempted him to jump ship and try his fortune in the diggings.

He had come across the whore as she being flogged by the brothel keeper. The Irish sailor had taken the whip and used it on the brothel keeper. Being a big man and overly strong, he had been a mite too enthusiastic and the beaten man never recovered from the assault.

The union of sailor and the whore had resulted in Douglas Earl. He had survived a rough childhood to become a giant like his father with the broad flat face of his mother.

Now Douglas Earl sat and drank whiskey in Devil's Kitchen, one of the two taverns operating in Jarrod's Cross. He drank whiskey and watched and waited. He was waiting for someone in particular.

And then the man he was waiting for walked through the door.

Travel stained with several days' growth of beard, the Mortimers pushed through the batwings and stood just inside the saloon. The place was crowded. A melodeon jangled out, competing with the din of conversation. Tobacco smoke hung low in a permanent fog within the big room.

The newcomers seemed overwhelmed by the noise, lights and smells. For a few moments they stood and let the warmth and hullabaloo sweep over them. The brothers looked towards their parent and leader. He pursed his lips and nodded.

Grinning widely, his sons elbowed a path to the bar

where two sweating bartenders laboured over the task of providing a seemingly never-ending stream of drinks to thirsty customers.

The Mortimers were flush with the money from the bank raid. They had also looted the bodies of the dead posse, taking wallets, cash, rings and watches. This was the money they were intent on spending tonight.

Loaded with bottles and glasses and expensive cigars, they looked around for a table. Just then a fight broke out over a card game. Seizing the opportunity, the Mortimers grabbed the abandoned table while the former occupants were beating the hell out of each other. Owen Grendon had gone off on an errand of his own but expected to join them later.

The brothers grinned and toasted each other and relaxed. This was when they reaped the rewards of crime. They were looking forward to a good time, drinking whiskey and smoking expensive cigars and later in the evening bolstered up with alcohol they would take a trip to the whorehouse.

The melodeon played on, the cigar smoke rose to thicken the fog, the whiskey tasted good and they were alive to raid another bank another day.

'You're a lowdown snakebelly, Mortimer. Your mother was a mudsill and your father was a bottom feeder.'

The voice was low and guttural but loud enough for the Mortimer brothers to hear. They looked up swiftly to see the huge shape behind their dad. The Bowie held against Artie Mortimer's neck looked as long as a sword. Hands slid down to gun butts.

'Those boys as much as twitch an' they'll be burying you minus your head.'

'What the hell you want?' Artie ground out, and in spite of the threat there was no trace of fear in his voice.

'I want that five dollars you cheated me outa in that poker game down in Pallmatto. I've bin followin' your skunk smell ever since.'

'Poker game . . . what the hellaya talkin' about? What poker game?'

'Stand up real slow an' face me like a man. Don't make any sudden move.'

The boys were watching their pa – awaiting a signal to blast the stranger to hell. But with a razor-sharp blade making an indent in his neck it was too risky to try anything.

Slowly the senior Mortimer stood. The Bowie remained steady. Carefully he turned and saw the huge shape of Duglas Earl.

'You bastard, you black bastard. I'm gonna take that Bowie and shove it so far up your mulatto ass it'll come outa your ear.'

To the astonishment of the young men the big blade disappeared and Artie Mortimer and the man-mountain lounged towards each other. They grappled and hugged and slapped each other and chuckled.

'Boys, meet the meanest, orneriest killer this side of the Rio Grande.' Mortimer introduced the knife man. 'Douglas Earl. If'n he asks to play cards say no.'

Chairs were rearranged and the big man joined the party.

'These your boys, Artie? Shore a fine brood you got here. Is Owen with you by any chance?'

'Sure is, Douglas. He'll be joining us shortly.'

Bull, who considered himself a big man, felt dwarfed

by this giant. Even sitting, he looked taller than the average man. He offered Earl a cigar while Artie filled a glass with whiskey.

'You didn't by any chance have anythin' to do with that business down in Roanville?' the mulatto asked shrewdly as he lit the long cigar from Bull's half-smoked one.

'Kee-rist!' Artie Mortimer exclaimed. 'Has news of that reached here already?' He shook his head in disgust. 'That telegraph wire is bad news for us gentlemen of the road. Mebbe we shoulda cut the dangblasted thing afore we lit out. Mind you,' he grinned, 'we was in a mighty big hurry. Owen caught a slug in the shoulder. Had to rescue him from the gawddamned posse.'

'The thing about you, Mortimer, is you look after your own.'

Artie grinned again at the big man. 'We all need a helpin' hand now an' then. Remember that time I hauled your ass outa that Yankee prison.'

'Will I ever forgit? You dang near blew me to kingdom come when you dynamited that gate.'

Artie roared with laughter. 'I was never too good with explosives. Man, when you came outa that jail you had more plaster on you than a elderly whore.'

'M' ears didn't work for a month of Sundays after that. In fact I don't think they ever worked proper since.'

'What's that?' yelled Artie, and slapped the table while the butt of the joke chuckled deep in his chest. The giant rocked back and forth while his chair groaned dangerously under the weight.

'Son of a gun.' Owen Grendon came across and punched the big man on the shoulder. Earl jumped to his feet and made as if to give Grendon the same back-slapping treatment he had given Artie Mortimer.

'Whoa, whoa,' Owen protested, 'cain't you see I'm walkin' wounded?' Indeed, his arm now rested in a nice new sling. 'I bin to see the sawbones. Says as I needn't worry about infection or anythin'. Tole me to take a fortnight off work.' He grinned at his companions. 'When he asked me what line of work I was in, I tole him bankin'. He says . . . he says as . . .' Owen had difficulty containing his mirth sufficiently to deliver the punch line. 'He says as bankin' ain't too onerous, mebbe I just need to take it easy for a few days.'

The whiskey flowed – the cigars burned slow and satisfying and old friends caught up on news of comrades.

'What brung you here, Douglas?' Artie finally asked.

Douglas Earl rolled the cigar around in his mouth and eyed Artie Mortimer. 'I was lookin' fer you,' he finally confessed.

'You was lookin' fer me? What is it? You need money? Just name it, ole buddy.'

The big man leaned forward and took up his whiskey glass. It was lost in his big hand. He took a slug and set the glass back on the table. Bull, who seemed fascinated by the giant, immediately refilled it. Douglas nodded his appreciation.

'Tom Percy,' he said simply.

Both Owen Grendon and Artie Mortimer turned their full gaze on Earl. The sons of Artie Mortimer sat still and carefully eyed the older men.

'What is it, Douglas? Something serious to bring you all the way out here to find us?'

Douglas took the cigar out of his mouth and vented a

long plume of smoke before replying.

'Tom Percy needs some help. He's run into a passel of trouble in a place called Lourdes, up north somewheres.'

For long moments Artie Mortimer stared at his old friend. At last he gazed around at his family.

'Have your fun tonight, boys. Come mornin' we're lightin' out for Lourdes. If Cousin Tom's got trouble then it becomes our trouble.'

18

Morgan sat on a big high-backed chair in the hallway, her arms wrapped around her body. She looked the picture of abject misery. Her hair was a bird's nest and her face was smudged with dirt and tears. Dressed in her male clothing she could easily have been mistaken for the original mad woman of the hills.

A door opened and Allison Grant emerged. Carefully she closed the door behind her. Morgan looked up and watched this beautiful woman walk toward her. Suddenly she was conscious of her own dishevelled appearance. Belatedly she drew her fingers through the dark tangled locks of her hair. The effect was negligible. She wished she had time to tidy herself. This charming woman made her feel like a piece of trash that had somehow been blown into her very clean and elegant home.

None of this showed in the demeanour of Allison Grant. As she approached the girl her arms were outstretched in greeting.

Morgan, who could swear a teamster into silence, could handle any team of oxen, horses or mules and could put a rowdy cowboy in his place with a look, shrunk back in her seat. She suddenly felt very self-conscious and wished she was anywhere than in the presence of this assured, older woman. Usually on top of any situation, she was feeling like a little girl caught in the act of wetting her pants in someone's front room.

Warm soft hands grasped her own work-hardened ones and Morgan was drawn up out of the chair. To her wonder and embarrassment Allison wrapped her arms around her and drew her close. Morgan could smell an elegant fragrance. She herself was dirty, smelly and uncouth but yet this supernatural being was folding her in her arms.

'My dear, my dear, thank you, thank you.'

Morgan could not stop the tears that spilled from her eyes. Suddenly the terror and fright of the day's events overcome her and she sobbed helplessly into Allison's soft, scented shoulder.

Morgan felt that by rights she should never have met, never mind be in the same house as this wonderful being. Yet here she was with her arms around Morgan as if it were the most natural thing in the world. She tried to bring her sniffles under control and drew back a little from the comforting embrace.

'How is he?' she whispered.

Allison took Morgan's face in her hands. She bent forward and in spite of the grime and smeared tears on the girl's face she kissed her. And Morgan felt fresh tears spill from her eyes.

'He's going to be all right. Doc McMurdo reckons with rest and care he'll be up and about again in no time. He's given him a sedative and he's sleeping peacefully. We're never going to be able to repay the debt to you for bringing him here. You saved his life. I'll be forever grateful to you, Morgan. Losing Hal would have left a terrible gap in this family. Now we must look after you.'

Morgan shrank back.

'Please, I'll be all right. I must go now.'

'You, young lady, are going nowhere till you have had a bath, rested and been fed. Now come along. How hungry are you?'

And Morgan who had not eaten for hours suddenly felt ravenous.

'I'm all right, really. I must get back to my folks.'

'Come,' Allison said imperiously and took Morgan by the arm. And Morgan who prided herself on her independence went along without further protest.

The older woman led the way downstairs and seated her in the dining-room. Morgan felt overwhelmed as she sat at the large pine table. She looked around her at the fine furniture and wall coverings. The Big G's unpretentious ranch house was like a palace to the girl who had spent most of her eighteen years in wooden shacks and sleeping rough in the backs of wagons.

'Melissa,' Allison called. 'Melissa.'

The cook came into the dining-room. Her eyes were swollen and she held her apron up and dabbed at her face.

'How is young Massa Hal, Mistress Allison? I's bin prayin' for him.'

Morgan stared at the young black woman. She realized the woman had been weeping. To her surprise Allison Grant put her arms round the cook and patted her back while laying her cheek against the woman's face.

112

'There, there, Melissa. Hal's going to be all right. Some rest and some of your good vittles is what the doctor says he needs.'

'Oh, praise the Lord, praise the Lord. I'll bake bread an' cookies an' make them there pancakes he likes so much.'

'I know you will, Melissa. Between us we'll make him well again. He's sleeping now and it'll be a while before he can take solid food. It'll be soup and broth for a while. But right now we have a young lady to feed.' She turned and indicated Morgan.

'Oh, missy,' the woman curtsied to the girl. 'You is the young 'un as brought Hal back to us. I'll cook you the best supper you ever eated. You is a angel. You is a angel sent from Heaven to this here house.'

'And, Melissa, get the kettles on. We need lots of hot water.'

'Yes, ma'am.' And Melissa, glad of something to keep her busy, retired to the kitchen to cook breakfast for the shabby, young woman who had brought her beloved Hal safe home again and to heat water for a bath.

Some time later, Morgan was in Allison's bedroom wrapped in a robe.

'But I got some new jeans in the wagon,' she was trying to tell Allison.

While she was in the bath – a luxurious new experience for Morgan more used to bathing in streams and rivers – her clothes had vanished.

'Nonsense, you might as well be comfortable.'

Allison was rummaging in the large wardrobe. Every now and then she would pick out a garment, glance over at Morgan, then come to some decision and rummage some more. The under garments were soft cotton. Then came the petticoats trimmed with lace. A bright green skirt with a beige blouse edged with a high lace collar was the final choice.

In spite of muted protests Allison applied herself to arranging Morgan's hair. After vigorous towelling she brushed out the tangles and arranged a simple green ribbon to keep the dark tresses in place. When Allison stepped back to contemplate the finished product the girl was surprised to see the woman's eyes mist over. Mutely she led the girl to the mirror.

Morgan stopped and stared at the image. She saw a strange young woman looking back at her. The woman in the mirror was extraordinarily beautiful. Morgan put out her hand and tentatively touched the glass.

'What have you done to me?'

Allison turned her round to face her. Morgan saw the tears welling in the older woman's eyes.

'Just look at you, Morgan. You're a beautiful young woman. I did nothing. It's amazing what a little soap and water can do. You saved my boy. No matter what I do, I will never be able to repay you for that.'

Then they were in each other's arms and stayed that way for long moments. A commotion downstairs with the slamming of doors brought them to their senses.

'I think the other members of my family have arrived,' Allison said wiping hastily at her eyes. 'Come.'

Morgan, strangely timid in her new finery allowed Allison to take her hand and lead her from the room.

19

The five heavily armed horsemen sat their mounts in the yard of the Big G. Holstered Navy Colts could be seen beneath their coats and the stocks of carbines poked out from saddle scabbards. As well as these weapons each man carried a shotgun slung across his shoulders. It was a formidable force by any standards and the grim faces of the men indicated the serious nature of their business.

Harry Grant stood on his veranda looking out at the group. He too was armed with holstered revolver and a Winchester dangled loosely in one hand.

'Gawddamn it, Harry, I ain't havin' you on this trip. I know you're a good man with a gun but I don't want any trouble if'n I can avoid it.'

Harry Grant stared up at Sheriff Rex Blunt with exasperation written all over his face.

'Hell, Sheriff, you know I need to sit in on this one. Those fellas have a lot to answer for.'

'No, Harry, an' that's final. I'm lookin' for the Mortimer gang. I cain't have you on some vendetta with the Percys. I don't want a war on my hands. Let me handle it my way. I don't want you goin' off half-cocked.

Now, I'm orderin' you to stay on your ranch. I don't wanna have ta serve a warrant on you as well as all this other trouble. I'll need your word you'll stay put.'

For moments the two men tried to outstare each other. Harry Grant was first to blink.

'Damnit, Sheriff, if'n anyone has cause for grief it's me. Them bastards about hung young Hal. They're camped on my land an' look like fixin' to stay.'

'That's exactly why I don't want you out there startin' no shootin' war. Let the law handle this. That's what my job is all about.' The sheriff spread his hands as he appealed to the angry rancher. 'Now, you just look after your family. No tellin' where them fellas is. They're vicious, mean bastards. Slaughtered near 'nough a whole posse down near Roanville. Found some of them tied to trees. They'd done some knife-work on them poor boys after shootin' up the posse. Just stay put an' keep your eyes peeled.'

For a moment Harry Grant hung his head and his lips tightened.

'You tell them low-life as they have a deadline. If'n they don't start movin' on soon I'm comin' for them.'

'Thanks, Harry; do this legal an' you an' me won't fall out.'

'Good luck, Sheriff,' Harry said sullenly, and as the sheriff and his posse wheeled around to leave he muttered under his breath.

As they approached the area around Potter's Creek Sheriff Blunt called a halt.

'Jim, you an' Biff unlimber them Greeners. Keep them pointed into the camp.' Two of the riders unstrung the shotguns and balanced them across their pommels.

116

'You two use the rifles. But no one do nothin' only on a signal from me. If anythin' happens to me, light out back to town. Now spread out. Don't bunch up when we git to that there camp.'

The Percys were well aware of the approach of the horsemen. Tom and Harrison stood in front of the half-finished timber building while the remainder of the crew was scattered around the camp.

The sheriff noted the proliferation of small arms and rifles amongst the cowboys. His face was grim as he rode up and stopped before father and son.

'Howdy, fellas, I'm Sheriff Blunt.' He glanced around the camp. 'You fellas look like you're expectin' trouble.'

'What you want, Sheriff? We ain't broke no laws,' Tom Percy answered.

'Well, that's not what I heard. Lynchin' a fella is agin the law.'

'Don't know nothin' about no lynchin', Sheriff. Who's bin lynched?'

'Fella by the name of Grant. Dad owns this land you're squattin' on. Which reminds me. He sends you fellas a message. Wants you off'n his land. Says as a deadline is set.'

'We got some sick stock an' a couple a fellas down with fever. We're just waitin' till they's fixed up, then we'll move. Cain't risk movin' them while they's poorly.'

'Um, well, that weren't what I come fer. Bunch of outlaws is on the loose an' reportedly movin' this way. The Mortimer Gang robbed a bank in Roanville an' wiped out a posse of lawmen. You seen anythin' of them?'

'Sheriff, why in hell's name would a bunch of outlaws

be interested in us? We're poor cattlemen. We ain't got nothin' worth stealin'.'

Sheriff Blunt sat his horse and scrutinized the two men in front of him. He was aware of the crew in the camp watching and listening to the exchange. There was a tension in the air that was almost tangible. He sensed these men were primed for trouble. One wrong move and it could end in a shoot-out. He wasn't too confident his little force would survive. And anyway that wasn't what he had come here for.

He had received Wanted posters for the members of the Mortimer gang. There was a $5,000 reward for each and every member of the gang. It was a tidy sum for a lawman to collect. Sheriff Blunt reckoned it would be a nice little nest egg for his retirement.

'Heard tell as you was related to these here Mortimers.'

'Mortimers . . . Mortimers . . .' Harrison Percy mused, 'there was some Mortimers distant related I think. Say, Pa, what about them Mortimers as used to hang out in the Killam Hills? Brewed some damned good corn whiskey. Was they related, Pa?'

'I ain't right sure, son. Might'ta bin on Aunt Gertie's side. I think her sister was married to a Mortimer. Or was it Morrison? Damned if'n I can remember right. What'd these fellas look like, Sheriff? Them as made the moonshine all looked like they was inbreedin' for generations – squinty eyes an' bow-legged and very hairy. Come to think about it they was the hairiest creatures I ever did see. An' the menfolk – they was just as bad. Ugly as sin . . .'

It was too much for the cowpokes. They began hooting and laughing and punching and slapping each other. The camp was in an uproar. Sheriff Blunt's face was getting redder and redder.

'All right, all right! It weren't that funny,' he bellowed, but his outburst only increased the mirth. 'If'n you see any strangers about just let me know. An' remember, git off the Big G range before trouble starts.' Angrily, the sheriff pulled his horse's head around. 'Come on,' he grunted to his riders. The laughter followed them as they rode away.

'I sure hope you weren't referrin' to me, you son of a bitch,' a mild voice queried from behind Tom Percy.

Tom turned and grinned at his cousin as he stood up from behind the half-built timber structure.

'Artie, I sure weren't referrin' to you. I knowed your ma. She was a racoon and your pa was a rattlesnake.'

The men grinned at each other.

'Well, at least I didn't have a sheep for a mother and a Mex for a father.'

'Why you son of a bitch, don't you insult my mother. She never lay with no Mex.'

The huge figure of Douglas Earl rose to stand beside Artie Mortimer.

'Anyone makes a remark about m' parents will find hisself talkin' to his belly button from the inside, for I'll shove his head up his ass.'

From the trees emerged the rest of the Mortimer gang in their familiar long leather coats. All were carrying rifles.

20

'What happened to your womenfolk? Didn't they come along on this trip?'

Tom Percy looked out into space before answering Artie Mortimer. 'We was hopin' to settle an' then send for 'em. Weren't sure how far we had to go to find a place. Glad they ain't here if'n there's fightin' to come.'

'I'd'a thought Morgan would have come along, at least. That daughter of yourn sure is a hellcat. Better'n any man I know with a wagon. Sure liked to watch her work that there bullwhip of hers.'

Harrison looked up with a scowl. He had been sitting beside the two older men working on a fragment of hide. In his hand was a piece of charcoal for he had been drawing a map. Before going into action Artie Mortimer wanted to know the terrain. He liked to plan meticulously for every eventuality. It was why he was so successful as an outlaw and why he had survived so long.

'Gawddamn woman,' Harrison snarled. 'We was hangin' Grant's son when she came by an' rescued him.'

Artie Mortimer looked from father to son. He noted Tom looked somewhat disconcerted.

'Morgan rescued Grant?' Artie suddenly grinned. 'Sure would like to hear this tale. Never a dull moment when Morgan's around.'

Harrison's scowl deepened. 'We had Grant strung up, figurin' it'd make his old man mad. Thought he'd come gunnin' for us. We could take him on on our own terms. Then Morgan rode up in that danged wagon an' cut him down. She lit out of here an' we ain't seen her since. Reckon she's holed up with the Grants.'

Mortimer raised his eyebrows and looked across at Tom Percy.

'That's about it, Artie. I weren't in favour of the hangin', but once Harrison's got the bit a'tween his teeth there ain't no stoppin' him. I didn't expect it to split my family.'

'Morgan snatched him.' Mortimer shook his head in admiration. 'You got two feisty youngsters, Tom. I must say I approve of what Harrison was doin'. Hurt a man's family an' he'll come at you hell for leather. Liable to make mistakes. As well as that it'd put the fear of hell into Grant's people. A frightened enemy is easier to fight.' He turned back to Harrison. 'How's that map comin' on?'

'Almost finished.' The youngster put the scrap of hide on the ground at Mortimer's feet. 'When our herd took off they ended up mixin' with the Big G. They got their crew workin' to separate the herds. We saw patrols of cowhands keepin' the two herds apart. Tole us to come an' collect an' then move on.' Harrison Percy pointed to a smudge on the outline map. 'This is where they're keepin' our cows. An' this here's the creek where we're camped. The Big G ranch is there,' he said pointing to a small square.

Artie Mortimer scratched at the stubble on his chin as he bent over the map. He looked up at Tom Percy.

'You still got that Hawken, Tom?'

'Sure, Artie. Wouldn't part with that.'

Some time ago the Mortimer gang had come across a hunting party of affluent businessmen. They had looted the camp and one of the prizes had been a Hawken sporting rifle complete with presentation case. Artie had given the rifle to Tom Percy as a gift. The rifle was one of Tom's treasured possessions and he used it occasionally to hunt buffalo and elk. He waited for Artie to explain his reasons for asking after the Hawken.

'I want you to ride around to the east. Git as near to the ranch buildin's as you need. Pump a few rounds into the place. You're not aimin' to hit anyone, but if you do it'll be a bonus. Then light outa there an' git back here. Try an' not let anyone see you, but that don't matter none.

'Harrison, you git a few men together. Then we'll ride over an' mix it with those Big G cowboys. Leave enough men here to guard your camp. Tell them to shoot anyone they don't recognize as tries to come in.'

'What about the Big G cows?' Harrison Percy asked eyeing the hawk-faced man. 'We could spare a few men to stampede those cows.'

'Leave them cattle alone. That's my reward. I figure on takin' those steers to market. I already got a buyer lined up.'

'Hell blast it,' Harrison exploded. 'We was figurin' on addin' them to our own herd. We lost a lotta head drivin' them this far and then with the stampede an' all. Was figurin' on makin' up our losses from the Big G stock.'

'Gawddamn it, Harrison, I'm here to help you git your hands on the Big G. I'm doin' it 'cause you're family. But I need somethin' for all the trouble I'm goin' to.'

'But that herd – it's all prime stock. It'd take years to build up to that again.'

'Don't push me, sonny. I ain't in the mood to haggle. Either we git our hands on that herd or we pack up an' ride outa here.'

'Pa,' Harrison appealed to Tom Percy, 'we gawddamn need that herd!'

Artie Mortimer stood and glared down at the red-bearded youngster. Harrison stood also and faced the older man. His face was flushed and angry looking.

'Make your play, sonny,' Artie Mortimer said in a low dangerous voice. 'Put up or shut up.'

For a moment the two men faced each other. There was a light of madness in the young man's eyes as he stared at his relation. Imperceptibly his hand crept towards his holstered gun. The tension grew. No one moved. No one made a sound. This was a battle of nerves between two strong-willed men. It would explode into violence or one of them would back down. The followers of both camps watched and waited. They would not interfere.

'Jesus Christ, Harrison, have you gone mad?' Tom Percy stepped in front of his son. 'Artie's come here to help us win a gawddamn ranch – the biggest, richest ranch in the county. What's a few gawddamn steers compared to that? Without Artie an' his gang we might as well pull up stakes an' creep from here with our tails a'tween our legs. For sure as shootin' that fella Grant won't be no pushover. At least we know we'll win with

Mortimer on our side.'

For a moment father and son stared eyeball to eyeball – the one anxious and pleading, the other quivering with barely suppressed anger.

'Son, listen to me. Don't go down this road. We need to stick together.'

Slowly the tension drained from Harrison. He threw up his hands and let them drop to his sides.

'Hell, Pa, I guess you're right. I sure had my heart set on them steers. What the hell, you can have the steers, Uncle Artie. We'll make do with the ranch.'

'Glad to hear that, son,' Mortimer replied laconically, relieved the crisis was resolved. He wouldn't have wanted to kill Tom's boy, but he wouldn't have backed down either.

'Right, back to business. How soon can your boys be ready to ride?'

'Any time soon. Whenever you're ready.'

'Tom, you git that Hawken an' light out straightaway. By the time this day's finished that rancher fella'll be wondering where the next gawddamn pile of shit is gonna hit him. After Tom's done his shootin' Grant'll need to leave people to guard the ranch for fear of an attack. That way he'll split his forces. Make it easier for us to pick them off.' He turned and yelled across at his sons.

They had been playing cards with Douglas Earl and Owen Grendon. 'Gawddamn it. I tole you not to play cards with that Nigra. How much you lost?'

The Mortimer boys looked at their father sheepishly but did not reply.

'I oughta whip your hides. Cain't you listen to

124

anything I say! Git on them nags an' let's ride. We're goin' huntin'. There's a bunch of vermin on this here range we gotta clear out.'

21

Harry Grant stomped around the ranch house straining at the leash. He was not happy to stand by idle while the enemy lurked at the gates. When Allison saw her husband about to depart the house she confronted him.

'For pity's sake, Allison, I have a ranch to run. There are a thousand and one things to tend to. I just cain't sit around here all day and wait for Sheriff Blunt to come back to me.'

It was only after she elicited his promise not to go near the Percys that she felt confident enough to let him leave.

'Don't forget if it wasn't for Morgan Percy, Hal would in all likelihood be dead now. We have to respect her wishes not to cause trouble for her family. The poor girl is in enough bother as it is. Let's not add to her unhappiness by causing any more distress for her.'

Harry Grant rode off, leaving his family unprotected but thinking nothing of that.

'You look like a sky pilot,' Morgan observed, and then giggled nervously.

'And you're an angel come to minister to me.' Hal's voice was a hoarse whisper. The sight of the white bandage his mother had wound around his neck had prompted Morgan's remark.

It was not quite noon but the sun beat down harshly. The veranda provided some shade for the youngsters. Neither Hal nor Morgan seemed to notice that when they were together like this Allison Grant made herself scarce. That Hal was madly besotted with the beautiful young stranger was obvious to anyone with half an eye.

Since arriving at the ranch with Hal in tow Morgan had been living at the Big G. Allison Grant had refused to allow her to leave. And Morgan herself was concerned about her reception by her brother if she returned there. She was torn by her loyalty to her family and the guilt of having defied them.

Rescuing Hal Grant had been a spontaneous act. There had been no time to think. She could not recall without a shiver the madness in her brother's eyes as he attempted to stop her. At least some good things had emerged from her actions. Hal was on the road to recovery and also with the help of Allison she had persuaded Harry Grant not to go off half cocked and raid the Percy camp.

The two youngsters were inevitably thrown together. Hal was still weak from his near death ordeal and Morgan found herself in the unfamiliar role of nursemaid.

'What's gonna happen, Hal? Your father ain't one to take things lyin' down.'

Hal looked at the worried frown of the girl who had saved his life. He had fallen for her in dusty jeans and driving an ox-drawn wagon. Now he felt a constriction in his chest every time he looked at her. Jokingly he claimed his mother had roped a maverick and tamed her.

Dressed in a simple blue cotton dress and her hair tied with a ribbon she did indeed look like a lovely vision of an angel. Only he recollected most images of angels had blonde hair. However, none of the pictures in the family Bible and holy books came anywhere near the breath-taking beauty of Morgan.

'I don't honestly know, Morgan. Pa's pretty riled up. I feel only Ma is keepin' him from goin' agin your family out at Potter's Creek. And she told me he was beholden to you for savin' my life. How long that will keep him in check is anybody's guess. The trouble is your family is trespassin' on Big G land. At some stage they're gonna have ta move on. Whether they do it willin'ly or be kicked out seems to be the way of it.'

Morgan's face was troubled. 'Harrison . . . he ain't how I remember. He allus protected me. Pa was mostly away. After the war the government made things hard for Confederates. Pa couldn't farm an' had to go on the run from time to time. Harrison was left in charge. He was so young – too young to have such a responsibility. I think it hardened him – made him bitter.' Tears suddenly welled. Morgan fiercely fisted them away, turning her face from Hal as if ashamed of her weakness.

'We'll look after you, Morgan. Ma's real fond of you. She sure likes havin' you around.'

'You don't understand, Hal. I never lived much in a proper house. I feel like a misfit. Wearin' these nice clothes an' like doin' female things, it's all natural to your Ma. She's used to nice things. I worry about breakin' somethin', or gittin' dirty or . . . or . . . Oh Hal, I think I'd be happier behind a team of mules.' Her distraught eyes stared out at him. 'My granma used to say, if'n you put a silk coat on a goat it's still a goat . . .'

The crashing noise and scream from inside the house interrupted whatever reassurance Hal was about to give. For a frozen moment the youngsters stared at each other then simultaneously rose and rushed inside. Even as they blundered through the hall the brutal crash came again. The shrieking continued.

'The kitchen,' Hal shouted, and they hastened towards the source of the screaming.

Hal took in the smashed window and glass littering the worktop. Melissa was curled in a ball in a corner, her high-pitched screaming unabated. Even as they moved across to the cook the crash came again and a moment later the dull boom of a rifle.

'Christ, someone's shootin' at us!' Hal exclaimed in his curiously hoarse voice. He crossed quickly to the screaming woman.

'Melissa, Melissa, where'ya hurt?'

Morgan was beside him and quickly knelt.

'Melissa.' She grasped the cook by the arm and tried to turn her over. There was blood on the floor.

The terrible crash came again from another part of the house. Leaving Morgan to attend to Melissa, Hal ran back out into the hall. He grabbed a rifle from the rack and rushed outside.

Knowing the shots were coming from the back he ran around the side of the house. Sweat was breaking out on his body. Even this short activity stretched his limited energy. Another shot smashed into the building.

Hal glanced at the house. Every window was smashed. Rage burned in him giving him strength of purpose. He ran out towards the trees that had been planted many years ago by his grandfather, Big John Grant. It was a mature plantation now and the trees provided shelter from the winds that blew in from the east.

Within the trees Hal stopped. He stared out across the flat grasslands, rifle gripped ready to use. Slowly he traversed the horizon. There was nothing to be seen. He peered hard. Then he saw it. Far out in the distance – a tiny dot moving away. He raised the rifle. This was impossible. Surely even the swiftest steed could not run that fast after shooting up the house.

Knowing it was a waste of bullets he fired off his rifle. It did nothing to relieve his feeling of helplessness. Someone had shot into his home. A young woman lay wounded by the cold-blooded behaviour. Feeling frustrated and angry he returned to the house.

'How is Melissa?'

'She'll be all right. More scared than anything else. Once I removed the sliver of glass from her hand and put a dressing on it she calmed down. She was convinced she'd been shot.' Allison looked around at the subdued little family group gathered in the dining-room.

'Who would do such a thing?' John looked up at his father as he spoke.

Harry Grant speared a hunk of bread before replying.

'I don't know but I can make a shrewd guess. All this trouble started when a certain party set up camp on Big G land.' He deliberately did not mention the Percys by name but everyone at the table, including Morgan, knew exactly who he was talking about.

'How did they shoot from so far away,' Hal asked. 'By the time I got around the back they musta bin more'n a mile away.'

'Huntin' rifle. I dug one of the bullets outa the wall. Big piece of lead from a Sharps or the like. You could hit the side of a house with one of those,' Harry Grant answered laconically. 'The marksman was good. He put a shot into every window out back. Was fortunate no one was hit. Just a cut hand for poor Melissa.'

Morgan hung her head. She remembered the Hawken that belonged to her father. Her face burned with shame as she compared this decent family with her own wild kinsmen.

Any further introspection was interrupted by a commotion out in the yard. The men leapt to their feet and ran into the hall. A few moments were lost as they fumbled for weapons from the gun-rack.

Boots thudded on the boards outside followed by a thunderous knocking on the front door.

'Mr Grant, Mr Grant!' a voice bellowed out. 'Mr Grant, come quickly.' The banging on the door echoed through the house like the drums of doom.

22

'Jeez, man it was terrible. They just rode up an' started shootin'. Must'a bin a dozen of 'em. Matt Timpson was hit straight off. Then Bob Burton went down. Luke got hit. I didn't see no more, Mr Grant. I lit out of there as fast as Trex could run. I guess I was one of the lucky ones. I run Mr Grant, but there were nothin' else to do. I mean . . .' The cowboy trailed off embarrassed and ashamed.

'Christ, Ted, you did right,' Harry Grant reassured him. He reached over and patted the man on the shoulder. 'Someone had to bring us the news. You did well, Ted. You did real good.'

But the cowboy's haunted eyes told a different story. He had run out on his pals. It burned a deep stain of shame inside. It wasn't an easy thing for him to adjust to.

'Did you recognize any of 'em?'

The man shook his head. 'They was all strangers. The ones as did the shootin' wore them long leather coats. They were leading the gang.'

'Well, it doesn't take a lot of figurin'. I have a shrewd guess who's responsible. The same bunch as shot up the house earlier today.' Harry Grant looked around him. 'Right, we'd better git out there. See if'n we can help anybody.' Harry Grant turned to his son. 'John, git a wagon rigged. We might have ta bring back the bod—' He stumbled for a moment over the words '. . . bring back the wounded.' As John left the room Harry Grant turned to Allison, standing white-faced. 'We'll bring 'em back. He's probably all right.' He was referring to Luke Parsons, the ranch foreman. Luke was Allison's brother.

Pa,' John had returned. 'We ain't got no one to take out a wagon. All the hands were out working.'

'I'll do it. I'll git the oxen hitched up.' Before anyone could object or comment Morgan disappeared through the door.

Everyone piled out the door after her. Hal was in the hallway buckling on his gunbelt.

'Hal, what the hell ya doin'?' Harry asked.

'Gittin' ready to ride out with you, Pa.'

'No! You ain't fit yet. You stay here an' look after the house. They might come back here again. You stay here.'

For a moment it looked as if Hal was going to object. Then he nodded. 'OK, Pa, I guess you're right. I'll stay. No tellin' what that bunch of madmen is gonna do next.'

For those left behind at the ranch house it was a fraught time of uncertainty. Hal would have preferred to ride out with his father and brother. The uncertainty and boredom of waiting made him restless. He made several circuits of the house, peering out through the ruined windows constantly on watch for unfamiliar riders or movement.

Allison stayed with Melissa. The weight of a revolver she had secreted pulled at her dress pocket. The weight

133

of dread felt even heavier as she waited the return of the rescue party.

It was Hal who spotted the riders and wagon.

'They're comin' in, Ma,' he yelled, and ran out on to the yard to greet them.

Allison joined him, the feeling of dread building in her breast. When she saw her husband's face she gave a little involuntary sob.

Morgan, her face drawn and pale brought the wagon to a halt before the house. She did not climb down but sat staring, a vacant look on her face.

The bodies were off-loaded and laid on the boards of the veranda. One groaning man was lifted out of the wagon and carried into the house. After that initial breakdown Allison remained calm.

'I'll look after Les,' she said, and followed the men ferrying the wounded man inside. There was a grim silence as the remaining hands gathered around.

'All of them, Pa?' Hal was round-eyed as he spoke to his father.

Harry Grant shook his head warningly at his son and nodded towards the wagon. Hal turned and noticed Morgan sitting hunched over the reins. He climbed on to the wheel and took her arm.

'Morgan, come in the house.' He led her unresisting inside.

Before Harry Grant followed he turned to the few hands left standing in the yard. 'Come in the house, fellas. Let's git you a bite to eat.'

The men filed inside after their boss. They crowded into the kitchen. It was a very subdued gathering.

Harry poured coffee from the big pot that stood

constantly on the stove. Allison had left a pan of stew ready. One of the hands took it on himself to dole out the food. The men fell to greedily. They had been out since before sun-up and were ravenous. Hal arrived back in the room and crossed to his father.

'Morgan told me some of what happened,' he said to his dad.

Harry Grant's face was grim. 'They killed about everyone. Les Jones was still hangin' on. You seen what he was like when we brought him in. He told what happened. When they were done shootin' they finished off the wounded. Left Les alive but with a bullet in him. He was to give me the message.'

'What message, Pa?'

Harry Grant turned bleak eyes on his son. Hal was his heir. One day the Big G would be his. Now all that was under threat.

'I was to pack my belongin's an' light outa here. Me an' my family would not be harmed if'n I pulled out.'

'Jeez, Pa. It were the Percys, weren't it?'

'They brung in help. They've teemed up with the Mortimer gang. A real mean outfit that's killed an' robbed across four states. They want me to meet them in Lourdes. I've to come in tomorrow and give them my answer.'

Father and son stared at each other. The men around the table had stopped eating. They watched the exchange between the Grants.

Harry Grant they knew as a strong man and fair boss. Whatever way he jumped they would jump with him. None of them rated the son, Hal. They knew his reputation as a wastrel. He would count for nothing. Harry was

135

king. His decision would decide their future. Whatever he determined they would follow him come hell or high water.

The yell from outside startled them all. Harry leapt to his feet. He had not thought to leave a guard outside.

'Halloa the house, Sheriff Blunt here. We're comin' in.'

The tension went out of the room as men relaxed. Harry strode out followed by his two sons.

'We thought we heard shootin' earlier on. Was tryin' to track it down.' Sheriff Blunt dismounted as he spoke. 'Don't suppose there's coffee on the go?' The sight of the tarpaulin-wrapped bundles on the stoop brought him up short. 'Looks like you can tell us all about that there shootin', Harry.' He mounted the few steps and stood beside the Grants. 'Who is it?'

'Luke Parsons, Ted Williams, Mat Timpson, Todd Johnstone, Bob Burton. Les Jones is inside bad wounded.'

'Jeez, Harry. All of them! An' Luke. How'd it happen?'

'Come inside, Sheriff.'

In moments the veranda was empty except for the ominous bundles laid out to one side. Harry Grant would have to bury his wife's brother and the hands that had died with him. Before that happened he had to decide what to do about the men who had brought so much death to the peaceful range of the Big G.

23

As Sheriff Blunt led his men into town the streets were strangely empty. The riders pulled up at the jailhouse and dismounted.

'Keep your eyes peeled,' the sheriff warned his deputies.

It was an unnecessary warning for each man was keyed up and watchful. They were all familiar with the Mortimers' reputation for treachery and ambush. Particulars of the butchery of the Roanville posse had filtered out. The gruesome details somehow grew with each retelling. Now the killers had struck closer to home.

The group filed inside the jail. Blunt had left a deputy in charge of the office while he was out on patrol. The man looked up as his boss strode inside.

'Chief, am I glad to see you. Bunch of mean *hombres* rode in an' took over the Hot Spur. Won't let no one leave.'

The sheriff did not reply immediately. He reached into the desk and retrieved a pipe. Placing it in his mouth he blew into it. Satisfied, he turned to his deputy. 'Any tobacco, Tim?'

His deputy reached over a tobacco sack. In silence the men inside the jail watched as the sheriff filled and lit his pipe.

'These fellas still down there?' Sheriff Blunt blew out a long plume of smoke.

'They're still there,' the deputy answered.

Sheriff Blunt took a long draw from his pipe before setting it down on the desk. 'Right, I guess we'll go down there and have a word.'

As the sheriff walked down the street the Big G riders pulled up at the livery yard.

Harry Grant peered down the street at the group of lawmen. Sheriff Blunt had asked Harry to allow him time to talk to the Percys. He had hoped to talk some sense into the mavericks and avoid trouble.

'Gawddamn, Sheriff, might as well talk to a bunch of wolves an' ask them not to molest the sheep,' he muttered. But he had promised the sheriff he would lay-off till the lawman had made his parley. He looked around at the half-dozen men who had chosen to ride with him. 'OK, boys, let's unsaddle. We'll give Blunt his chance.'

'When we git inside, spread out along the back wall,' Sheriff Blunt instructed his deputies. They still carried their shotguns. 'But don't do any shootin'. If there's trouble I'll give the signal. Mebbe I can settle this without a gun battle.'

He pushed inside the Hot Spur. His men piled in behind him and did as he instructed, lining up along the back of the saloon. They held their shotguns at waist height aimed into the room.

Sheriff Blunt spied the younger Percy playing cards with four or five other men. He looked around the saloon. There was an air of tension in the room. Men glanced uneasily at the sheriff. Behind the bar he saw two bartenders he did not recognize. They wore the usual aprons of their trade. One wiped at the bar top while the other was polishing a glass with a cloth. When he saw his men in position he walked across to Harrison Percy.

'Howdy, Sheriff,' the red-bearded youngster greeted him affably. 'You catch up with them mean Mortimers, yet?'

'Not yet, but it's only a matter of time. I came here to see you.'

The young man placed his cards on the table. 'What about, Sheriff? Tole you all I know.'

'Someone shot up the Big G yesterday. Several hands dead. Has all the hallmarks of Mortimer. Left a message for Harry Grant. Was to meet up with him here. I've come to see if 'n this thing can be settled peaceable.'

Harrison Percy leant back in his chair. 'Where is Grant? Ain't he with you?'

Something warned Blunt. It may have been the way Harrrison's eyes slithered sideways or the way he spoke. His eyes flicked around the saloon. On impulse he drew his revolver. A movement behind him drew his attention towards the bar. Where there had been two barmen now there were four. One of them was a huge black man. The four Spencers they held were pointed not at him but at the back wall where his men had positioned themselves.

He started to yell a warning when a movement at the table drew his attention. A young blond man was grinning at him over a Colt revolver.

'Howdy, Sheriff. I'm Dick Mortimer. I believe you was looking for me.'

His bullet took the sheriff high in the chest. Sheriff Blunt staggered back under the impact. His shouted warning died in his throat. The revolver in his hand felt heavy as he tried to raise his hand. His eyes were going out of focus. A second slug took him in the shoulder. As he collapsed he could hear the Spencer rifles booming out.

'Gawd . . .' he managed to groan, before he hit the floor.

'Jesus!' Harry Grant swore as the shots rang out. He headed up the street at a run. His men were seconds behind him. 'Gawddamn murderin' bastards!'

Harry could not quell the bad feeling in the pit of his stomach. He stumbled in the rutted roadway and almost went down. At the same time a rifle boomed out. He heard the man behind him give a yell. Harry swivelled round and saw Joe Greer slowly topple backward. There was a large hole in Joe's chest. Joe looked faintly surprised. His eyes fixed on Harry and then suddenly he collapsed – his body raising a small dust cloud as he hit the roadway.

'Git under cover!' Harry managed to yell as he dived for the boardwalk.

The rifle boomed again. Harry rolled hard against the wall of the building. The breath was momentarily knocked out of him. He heard that terrible booming sound as the rifle fired again. But an overhang hid Harry from sight of the gunman.

He glanced hurriedly into the roadway for his men.

They had scattered and gone to ground. Joe Greer lay sprawled like a straw dummy – a great hole in his chest. A mass of blood stained the dead man's shirt.

'Stay put,' he yelled to his men and drew another shot. It clipped the boardwalk in front of him. 'Can you see anything? Where's he shootin' from?'

'Cain't see a thing, boss. He's firin' from a window or rooftop.'

'Gawddamn it, he's got us pinned down.'

There was no reply. An unfamiliar stillness had descended on Lourdes. The town that normally should have been bustling with wagons and horses and people was like a ghost town. Nothing moved in or out. After the initial explosion of sound the shooting from the Hot Spur had gradually petered out.

Harry wondered what had happened to Sheriff Blunt. He feared the worst. The sheriff should have contacted him before now. He would have to flush out that gunman.

Harry removed his hat. Slowly he edged it as far ahead as he could. Using his revolver he nudged the brim slowly outwards. Harry almost jumped out of his skin as the rifle boomed out and wooden splinters flew through the air. He rolled out from cover and aimed his Colt skywards.

Anxiously he scanned the area he figured the shots were coming from. Even though he could see nothing of significance he began firing. Then he saw the telltale shift of movement from the roof of the Hot Spur. He emptied his revolver into that area of the roof and rolled back under cover. Perspiration leaked from his hairline and ran down his face. His clothes felt sticky from sweat.

'He's holed up on the roof of the Hot Spur. If 'n you can shoot into the fascia might just hit something,' he shouted across the street to the men flattened against the buildings on that side. 'But be careful. It's the son of a bitch with the huntin' rifle.'

Harry wondered if he had hit anything. From across the street his men fired a few shots and when the big rifle replied he had his answer.

24

'Stay here with the horses,' Hal instructed his brother. 'I'll find out what's happenin'. He looked up the street and saw the horses tethered outside the sheriff's office. The town was unnaturally quiet.

Men looked up apprehensively as he entered the Mule's Head.

'Hal, good to see you.' Falmouth was seated at a table, playing cards with his cronies. 'Come an' join us for a drink.'

'Jeez, Jack, ain't got time for that.' Hal stood by the table. 'I need some help. My family's got trouble. Passel of outlaws came by an' killed half-a-dozen of our riders includin' Uncle Luke. Pa's to meet them at the Hot Spur. There's gonna be a shoot-out. We're outnumbered, but Sheriff Blunt is gonna negotiate. I think it'll still come to a shoot-out. Sure wish I could sit in on it, but Pa gave me instructions to stay at home, gawddamn it.'

'Dang my britches, Hal. You sure come to the right person. Jack Falmouth never let a fella down yet. You say they's down at the Hot Spur.' Falmouth stood up. 'Here's m' gun.' He lifted a gunbelt from his chair and struggled to fasten it round his middle. His enormous belly was getting in the way.

'Massa Hal.' No Account had been leaning on a broom watching the card game and listening to Hal. 'You need to git in the Hot Spur?'

'Cain't, No Account. I shouldn't even be in town. If'n Pa sees me anywhere near the Hot Spur he's gonna be real mad.'

No Account liked Hal. The youngster had never looked down on him because of his lowly position or his colour.

'I git you in the Hot Spur, Massa Hal.' The swamper put one finger to the side of his nose and winked. 'Got m' own way of gittin' in an' out of that place.'

Hal turned his gaze on him. 'You sure?'

'Sure I'm sure! Follow me.'

'Hang on there, No Account.' Hal went to the front entrance. 'John, tie up them horses. We got a way to deal ourselves in the action.'

As the brothers followed No Account, Hal called over his shoulder for Falmouth to hurry.

'You go on, Hal. I'll follow as soon as I git this here gun belted on.'

Falmouth watched the brothers go then gave up on his gunbelt. He eased his fat bulk back into his seat. 'Plenty of time, Hal boy. Plenty of time for another drink.' He reached for the bottle on the table.

Outside the rear of the Hot Spur saloon, No Account pointed to the dilapidated wooden steps creeping up the full height of the building. 'Careful, Massa Hal. Some broke steps.' Then he began to ascend.

When the shooting from inside the saloon thundered out Hal jumped and put his foot on a rotten step. He

144

would have fallen only No Account caught him by the shoulder and steadied him.

'Jeez, Hal.' John turned scared eyes on his brother. 'Waddya think. . . ?' Even out back the gunfire sounded thunderous.

Hal said nothing. He motioned his guide to proceed. For some unknown reason No Account still carried his broom. Even with the gravity of the situation Hal had to fight down his giggles.

The shooting had quietened down to a few intermittent bursts. Then from above came the distinctive boom of a hunting gun. Hal's giggles died as quickly as they had risen.

'Keep goin', he motioned to No Account.

Now that the gunfire masked any noise they might make they went more swiftly up the rickety steps. The gunman on the roof kept up a steady pattern of shots. No Account poked his head above the roof level. Hal pushed up beside him. The rifle boomed out again and Hal heard someone shouting down in the street. He wasn't sure but it sounded like his father.

The gunman was crouched behind the wooden fascia. Hal saw him sighting down the rifle barrel into the street. In his haste to get on to the roof Hal missed his footing and tumbled on to the boards. The man swivelled his head and seeing Hal sprawled on the roof began to swing the long barrel around.

Falling awkwardly, the youngster was having difficulty finding his holster. The black nozzle of the big gun was aimed straight at Hal. For a moment the marksman watched the boy. Suddenly he grinned and Hal recognized him.

'Mr Percy,' Hal stuttered.

'Mr Percy, indeed. And you're the Grant whelp. Good bye, Master Grant.' Tom Percy grinned. 'You bin hangin' about too long.'

The broom came from nowhere. It flew like a spear accurate and straight and hit Tom Percy in the teeth. The gun in his hand went off. Hal felt something snatch at his ear. His Colt was out and bucked in his hand as he fired.

Tom Percy stepped back as the bullets struck home. He opened his mouth that was already bloody from the blow from the broom. The backs of his legs were hard against the fascia. He teetered on the edge. The Hawken slipped from his hands as he lost control. More bullets came from the street striking him in the back and then he toppled over and disappeared from view.

Hal stared at the empty space for moments.

'Yo all right, Massa Hal?' No Account was kneeling beside him.

'Jeez, I . . . I think so . . .'

'Your ear is bleedin', Massa Hal.'

Hal put his hand to his ear and felt the wetness. 'Just a scratch, No Account.' Suddenly he was grinning at the man. 'Where'd you learn to handle a broom like that?'

At that moment John poked his head over. His eyes opened wide as he regarded his brother.

'Jeez, Hal, you're bleedin'. What happened?'

Hal turned and pointed to the big rifle lying on the roof.

'I figure that's the rifle used to shoot up our house.' Suddenly he went very still, his eyes staring vacantly out into space.

'Hal, Hal, you all right?'

Hal turned and looked at his brother. 'John, that was Tom Percy. I just killed Morgan's pa . . .'

John reached out and gripped his brother's shoulder. 'Hal, that was the fella as tried to hang you. An' by the look of all that blood he dang near finished the job. You ain't got nothin' to regret.'

'Tha's right, Massa Hal. It were him or you.'

Hal blinked and turned to No Account. 'Where do we go from here?'

The man pointed to a trapdoor in the corner of the roof. It was propped open, evidence of how the sniper had reached the roof. He picked up the Hawken.

'Guess he won't be needin' this no more.'

They climbed down the creaking ladder and on to the landing that led to the bedrooms. This was where the women entertained the clients. Right now it was empty and silent. The three men crept to the balcony. Both Hal and John gaped at the scene revealed. The floor of the Hot Spur was like a battlefield with bodies strewn everywhere. The boys had never seen so much blood.

'Son of a bitch. They've killed Sheriff Blunt,' Hal whispered. 'An' those must be his deputies. Jesus H. Christ.'

It was an appalling sight for the two youngsters. Someone was shouting from the street.

'Sheriff Blunt, this is Harry Grant out here. What's happenin'?

Hal watched the men below. They were in a huddle discussing something. He recognized Morgan's brother. The bearded youngster pointed upstairs. A man detached from the group and came over. He began to ascend the stairs. No Account jerked his head towards

147

the bedrooms. They tiptoed across the landing and pushed inside.

Hal kept the door open a crack so they could watch the man coming up the stairs. 'Jesus,' he whispered. John was kneeling on the landing fiddling with his boot.

'What the. . . !' the man on the stairway pulled his pistol.

John looked up and smiled. 'Howdy, mister, what's all the shootin'? He rubbed his eyes. 'Gawddamn it, I'll never drink whiskey ever again.' John stood up.

'Gawddamn kid. What're you doin' here?' The man was hesitant, puzzled by the presence of the youngster.

'You won't tell my ma you seed me.' John moved to the head of the stairs. 'I ain't supposed to come in here.'

The man allowed his pistol to droop and half turned as if to call down to the men in the saloon.

He never saw the Bowie in John's hand. The boy drove the big blade hard into the man's belly. At the same time he swung him round and ran with him towards the door behind which his brother was watching. Hal was out in the corridor instantly, his hand clamped around the man's mouth. The trio wrestled desperately in the silent intimacy of steel and blood. The man's struggles grew weaker and weaker till finally his legs gave way and he subsided to the carpeted floor. The boys went down with him. They lay there bathed in sweat and blood – shaking and scared.

25

'Where in hell did you learn a trick like that?' Hal hissed at his brother.

John looked at him, his eyes wide and panicky. 'I . . . I just imagined he were a steer. I had to take him down hard and fast.' He looked wonderingly at the bloodied knife. 'I didn't even know I had the Bowie in my hand.'

'Come on.'

They crawled to where No Account was lying on the landing peering through the banisters. The Hawken lay by his side looking long and sleek and deadly against the carpeted landing.

'What's happenin'?'

No Account shook his head. 'There's folk on the outside an' folk inside. They's doin' a lotta talkin'.'

Hal studied the man who was shouting to the folk outside. He was a hawk-faced man wearing a long leather coat. Spread out around him were more men similarly dressed.

'We got the sheriff with a pistol agin his head. You

come on in where we can talk,' he yelled, and paused for a response.

'Why don't you come on out here in the street where I can see you?' came the shouted answer. Hal recognized his father's voice.

'Most of us is shot up,' the hawk-faced man responded. 'Dang blasted sheriff had his men with Greeners. They sure made a mess of'n us boys. We scared you gonna do the same to us if'n we come out there.'

The men in the saloon had Spencer rifles and they were all trained on the front entrance. Hal turned to John.

'Slide over on the other side of the stairs,' he whispered. 'Git that Winchester ready. If Pa comes through that door he'll be cut to pieces.' He turned to No Account. 'Are you in on this?' he asked.

For answer the black man slid the Hawken forward and cradled his cheek against the polished wooden stock. 'I's with you, Massa Hal.'

The exchange was still going on below.

'Sure wish Jack and his bunch git here soon,' Hal said.

'You is gonna wait a long time fo' Jack Falmouth, Massa Hal.'

Hal stared at No Account. 'Whaddaya mean?'

The white teeth flashed in No Account's face. 'Massa Hal', he said in a patient tone, 'you is sure one trustin' sonabitch. Jack Falmouth is out an' out coward. He not gonna risk his skin for his own mutha, an' you not even related.' He dragged the last word out long and slow.

Hal turned his attention back to the saloon. 'Thanks, No Acccount,' he hissed out of the corner of his mouth.

Now he knew they stood alone against the Mortimer gang and the Percys. Then he remembered Tom Percy toppling off the roof. 'Son of a bitch,' he muttered. 'Son of a bitch.'

The negotiations below had reached a climax.

'We're comin' in,' the voice yelled from outside, 'but no funny business.'

'All right, Grant. We just want a way outa this. You let us have a sawbones for our wounded an' our horses an' we ride outa this gawddamn town.'

The hawk-faced man turned and grinned at his companions. 'Let them inside afore you start shootin'.'

Hal stood on the top step of the stairs. He held his Colt pointed into the body of the saloon. The outside door began to slowly open. Hal hesitated, reluctant to start shooting. Then he remembered choking out his life on the end of a rope. He also remembered the screams of Melissa as the bullets thudded into his home. He steeled himself.

'Now!' He shot Artie Mortimer in the back of the head. Beside him the Hawken blasted out and the outlaws, masters of the ambush, found themselves the victims of such a practice.

Beside Hal, John opened up with the Winchester. The noise was deafening. Down in the saloon was a scene of mayhem and chaos. The outlaws were diving for cover and at the same time retaining enough presence of mind to shoot back.

Beside Hal splinters of wood flew from the wooden balustrade. Bullets thudded into the stairs. He seemed to bear a charmed life. Coolly he stood atop the steps and fired into the outlaws scrambling for cover. The skills he had honed on those long lonely hours firing at tin cans and wooden targets were paying off.

As his hammer clicked on an empty chamber the swing doors burst open and Harry Grant burst, in six-guns in hand. Behind him piled in the Big G hands revenge in their souls for murdered comrades. Battle was joined.

Hal stood on the top step and swiftly reloaded. Below him the battle raged. The outlaws taken by surprise and now receiving fire from front and rear were faring badly. Their Spencer rifles were not ideally suited to close quarter fighting. Harry Grant and his cowhands were taking a deadly toll of the outlaws. The gunmen below had no cover from the deadly hail of lead that No Account and John were laying down. Several bodies had joined the slain members of Sheriff Blunt's party in the sawdust.

One of the outlaws called out. 'Don't shoot, for Gawd's sake don't shoot.'

Three or four men raised their hands in a gesture of surrender. The shooting petered out. An awful silence seemed to descend on the room. Then a wounded man began groaning.

The tension remained. Hal's eyes raked the room. Slowly he descended. Harry Grant, his pistol trained on the defeated gunmen, glanced up at his son.

'I thought I told you to stay at the ranch.'

Hal stared blankly at his father. Before he could think of a response the doors burst open and a fat man waving a pistol waddled into the saloon.

'Gawddamn it, Hal, good job I came when I did. I'll kill any man as moves. I jus' shot a couple of fellas outside – lying out there in the street.'

From above Hal the Hawken boomed. The bullet chewed up the floor beside the newcomer. Jack Falmouth collapsed to the floor with a groan.

'My Gawd, my Gawd,' he screeched. 'Oh my Gawd. I'm hit. Help me, Hal. Help me. Please help me.'

Hal looked down at the fat man cowering on the floor. He turned and looked up at the gallery. White teeth gleamed down at him out of a dark face.

'No Account, if'n you ever want a job we could do with an extra hand out at the Big G.'

'Massa Hal, you jus' hired youself a top hand,' came the reply. 'Doan tell me I missed that tub o' lard.'

Hal turned back to his father, ignoring the blubbering fat man lying in the sawdust. 'Whaddaya want to do with these fellas, Pa?'

His father was staring down at the body of Sheriff Blunt.

'By rights we should string them all up.' Then he sighed. 'There's bin enough blood spilled. Disarm them an' lock them in the gaol. We'll wire Toska and git the marshal over to take care of things.'

Hal was walking around the saloon. 'That Harrison Percy, the one as hanged me. No sign of him.' He looked up at Harry Grant. 'I killed his pa. He was the one with the Hawken. But where's Harrison?' He swung round to the survivors of the shoot out. 'Where's Percy? He should'a bin here with you.'

A giant of a black man who had been leaning against the bar nursing a shattered arm spoke up. 'Son of a bitch gone out to your place. Afore you opened up, Artie tole Percy to light out for the Big G. Said fer him to kill every man, woman an' chil' on the ranch. That way there's no one to claim estate.'

Hal and Harry looked at one another. 'Jeez,' Hal let out his breath slowly. He was a step behind Harry Grant as they headed for the door.

26

Harrison Percy dismounted just outside the yard of the ranch house and tied his horse to a fence rail. The house looked deserted. Keeping his hand on his revolver he moved cautiously across the yard. No one challenged him as he ascended the steps to the veranda.

He tried the front door. It wasn't locked. He pushed it open and stepped into a hallway. Then he heard the sounds from down the hall. Carefully he tiptoed to an open doorway and peered through the opening. Inside were two women busy at separate tasks. Only then did he take out his revolver.

'Now ain't this a cosy scene?' he remarked casually as he stepped inside the kitchen.

The women looked up in some surprise.

'Howdy, Morgan. You seem to have settled in here. Don't you miss your old family?'

'Harrison!' Morgan stared round-eyed.

Harrison glanced at the older woman. 'You is a redhead jus' like me.' He indicated his own red beard. 'Mebbe that's why Morgan took to you.'

'What are you doing here?'

'I jus' stopped by fer to look over my new property.'

The look of contempt the woman gave him angered Harrison.

'Where is my husband?'

'You must be the bitch as whelped that pup Grant.' Harrison leaned against the door. 'Guess he's joined that sheriff fella on the floor of the Hot Spur.'

'You lie. Scum like you could never put my Harry down.'

'I guess there's only one way for you to find out, whore. You can join him.'

Harrison lifted the gun a fraction and fired. The woman staggered back and cannoned into the back wall. Convulsively her hands grasped the front of her apron. She slid down the wall staring in stupefied surprise at her assailant.

'No!' screamed Morgan. As her brother fired again she flung herself on top of the woman. The bullet struck the girl in the spine. Her back arched and her lips worked. A long strangled moan issued from the stricken girl. Her cry bubbled to a close and she sank on to the woman she was trying to protect.

'Jeez, Morgan!' Harrison's cry was a pitiful wail.

Blood made an ugly dark patch on Morgan's back. The older woman was moaning as her arms crept around the wounded girl. Harrison stared in mute horror at his handiwork. He lifted his free hand in a gesture of helplessness. 'Morgan,' he whispered and then heard the hoofs thumping into the yard and his head jerked up. He stood like that, frozen in place.

Footsteps thudded on the boards outside.

'Morgan, where are you?'

The look on Harrison Percy's face changed from that of anguish to one of fury. He turned and stepped into the hallway. Hal Grant was standing inside the front door in the act of calling out again. He stopped abruptly and slowly turned to face his enemy.

Allison Grant stared down at the ebony hair of the girl she had grown to love. She kissed the top of the girl's head. Slowly and with painful effort she eased the lifeless body to one side.

The bullet had struck her low down in the groin. The pain was dull and persistent. She slid her hand down and slipped it inside the big pocket in her apron. She felt the angular shape of the .44 she had been carrying around since this terrible trouble had started.

Grasping the gun she pulled the weapon free. She stared at the ruined handle. The bullet had smashed the polished walnut and bent the metal. The impact of the bullet striking the gun had knocked her down. There was no sign of any blood.

The man who had shot her and Morgan and claimed to have killed her husband had his back to her. Allison lifted the gun and cocked it.

'Wa-al, if'n the pup hasn't come home to Momma, with his tail a'tween his legs. Ain't gonna do you no good. I jus' put her out of her misery. She's gone to join your pa.'

'What have you done?' Hal's voice was almost a whisper.

'The Grant dynasty no longer exists. You're the only one left. It was good of you to come home. You can now join your family in Hell.' Just then Harrison heard the

157

unmistakable sound of a gun being cocked. For a fraction he looked over his shoulder.

Hal went for his gun. He knew he didn't stand a chance but his hand streaked down in the attempt to get his gun out and finish this feud. He heard the explosion of the gunshot and jerked convulsively. Beside him a lamp disintegrated. His own gun was out of the holster. He brought it up to firing position and squeezed the trigger.

The impact of the slug flung Harrison against the wall. Hal was poised for another shot as he watched the man slide to a sitting position. The bearded youngster was trying to bring up his gun. Slowly his hand slackened. The gun made a thumping noise as it hit the floorboards. Then Hal was pushed to one side as Harry Grant blundered past him.

The big willow tree was an enormous shape against the blazing summer sky. It had been left to grow without restriction and now reared up in a great cathedral of branches, leaves and sunlight. The tree was a haven to a multitude of wild life. It was beneath this weeping tree that Big John Grant, Hal's grandfather, had buried his wife. Years later he had been laid to rest beside her. The site had become the cemetery for the Grant family.

A crowd of people was now gathered before a row of fresh dug graves.

'We pray Thee, O Lord, to show Thy mercy towards Thy departed servants whose only desire it was to do Thy will. Let them be united with throng of the faithful. Through Thy mercy, may they join with the choirs of

SON OF A GUN

angels in heaven. Through Jesus Christ our Lord.'

'Amen,' responded the congregation.

In ones and twos the mourners began a slow drift towards the yard. Long makeshift tables covered in white sheets held the food for the funeral guests. The members of the Grant family lingered by the graves. Unable to contain himself Hal fell to his knees and drove his fingers into the earth on one of the graves. His tears fell freely.

'How can that preacher talk of a merciful God when He allows this to happen,' he wailed.

'Hal, Hal.' His mother reached for him and helped her son to his feet. 'Morgan gave us life in exchange for her own. But for her you would not be here and neither would I. Don't let her sacrifice be in vain. Give her a full life in exchange. Make your own life into her memorial.'

Harry Grant stepped forward. He looked into the stricken face of his son.

'Hal, I badly misjudged you. I believed you were a weaklin' and a wastrel. Then you did somethin' lawmen across the county failed to do: you wiped out the Mortimer gang. A man couldn't be prouder than I am of my son.'

'Pa,' Hal blinked away the tears, 'I had a bit of help. I couldn't have done it without John.'

Harry Grant reached out and pulled both his sons against him. 'Boys, you are the best of men.' He released his grip. 'Let's go and git some eats.'

Hal Grant half turned as he moved away with his family. He lifted his hand in a gesture of farewell – then he let it fall to his side.

The Grants walked down towards the yard of the Big

G. They had buried their dead and now they would go down and mingle with the mourners. In spite of the pain and grief in their hearts the living had a duty to carry on.